Maigret
and the
Toy Village

Maigret and the Toy Village

Georges Simenon

Translated by Eileen Ellenbogen

A HARVEST BOOK
A HELEN AND KURT WOLFF BOOK
HARCOURT BRACE & COMPANY
SAN DIEGO   NEW YORK   LONDON

Requests for permission to make copies of any part of the work
should be mailed to: Permissions Department,
Harcourt Brace & Company,
6277 Sea Harbor Drive, Orlando, Florida 32887-6777.

Library of Congress Cataloging-in-Publication Data
Simenon, Georges, 1903–1989
Maigret and the toy village.
Translation of Félicie est là.
"A Helen and Kurt Wolff book."
I. Title.
PZ3.S5892Maegwn [PQ2637.I53]   843'.9'12   79-1843
ISBN 0-15-155554-0
ISBN 0-15-655154-3 (Harvest: pbk.)

Printed in the United States of America

First Harvest edition 1987

B C D E

Maigret
and the
Toy Village

1

Peg Leg's Funeral

It probably did not last more than a second, but the impression it made upon Maigret was quite extraordinary. It was like one of those dreams that, we are told, pass in a flash but seem to go on forever. Years later, Maigret could still have pointed to the exact spot where it happened, the paving stone on which he had been standing, the stone wall on which his shadow had been projected. He would be able to remember not only every detail of the scene, but also the various smells in the air and the feel of the breeze, all of which vividly recalled his childhood.

It was the first time that year that he had ventured out without his overcoat, his first sight of the countryside at ten o'clock in the morning. Even his pipe, an unusually large one, seemed to taste of spring. There was a lingering nip in the air. Maigret walked along with a heavy tread, his hands in his trouser pockets. Félicie walked beside him, or, rather, a little ahead of him, since in order to keep up with him, she had to take two steps for every one of his.

Together, they drew level with a brand-new building of pink brick. In the window were displayed a few vegetables, two or three cheeses, and a string of blood sausages on a ceramic plate.

3

Félicie quickened her step, stretched out her hand, and pushed open the glass door of the shop. And it was then, evoked, no doubt, by the sound of the bell, that Maigret experienced the sensation that he was never to forget.

The shop bell was no ordinary bell. A cluster of thin metal tubes was suspended above the door, which, when opened, created a draft that caused the tubes to collide and emit a carillon of tinkling chimes.

Long ago, in Maigret's childhood, the pork butcher in his home village had completed the redecoration of his shop by installing just such a carillon.

And this was why, at this moment, for Maigret the present seemed suddenly in abeyance. How long this feeling lasted it was impossible to tell, but while it did, Maigret was genuinely transported to another time and place. It was as if he no longer inhabited the body of the thickset Chief Superintendent obediently trailing along behind Félicie.

The long-lost village boy, it seemed, was there on the spot, hiding somewhere, invisible, looking on, with laughter bubbling up inside him.

Well, really! It was all too ridiculous, wasn't it? Could anything be more out of place than that solemn, bulky figure of a man in the company of that caricature of a woman out of a children's book wearing that absurd red hat? And in such surroundings, too, flimsy and insubstantial as a toy village.

What was he doing there? Conducting an inquiry? Investigating a murder? Here and now, among brick cottages, pink as sugared almonds, with the air full of the twittering of small birds, the fields sprouting tender young green shoots, buds bursting into bloom all over the place, and even the leeks in the shopwindow looking as pretty as flowers?

Yes, he was often to recall this moment in the years to come, and not always with equanimity. For years and years afterward, one or other of his colleagues at the Quai des Or-

4

fèvres would pick on a brisk spring morning to remark, half seriously, half teasingly:

"I say, Maigret . . ."

"What is it?"

"Félicie is here!"

And he could almost imagine her standing there, with her slim figure, her quaint clothes, her big blue eyes, her supercilious nose, and, above all, her hat, that outrageous scarlet confection, perched on the top of her head and trimmed with a stiff, iridescent green feather.

"Félicie is here!"

Grrr! It was well known that the name Félicie had only to be spoken for Maigret to growl like a bear. And this was not to be wondered at, since Félicie had given him more trouble than all the hardened criminals brought to justice by the Chief Superintendent in his long career.

On this particular May morning, Félicie really was there, standing at the door of the little grocer's shop. The sign, MÉLANIE CHOCHOI, ÉPICIÈRE, in yellow lettering, was just legible beneath a couple of transparent stickers advertising a brand of starch and a metal polish. Félicie stood waiting for the Chief Superintendent to be so obliging as to rouse himself from his reverie.

At long last, he stirred, found himself back in the real world, and gathered up the threads of his inquiry into the murder of Jules Lapie, nicknamed Peg Leg.

Her sharp features overspread with an expression of mingled hostility and irony, Félicie was braced to meet his questions, as she had been since early that morning. Behind the counter stood Mélanie Chochoi, a pleasant little woman, with hands folded on a bulging stomach, contemplating the Chief Superintendent of the Police Judiciaire and Peg Leg's servant. And a very odd couple they must have seemed to her.

5

Maigret, puffing gently at his pipe, looked about him. His eyes wandered from the cans of food on the shelves to the unfinished street beyond the glass door, with its newly planted, spindly little trees. Taking his watch from his waistcoat pocket, he finally murmured, with a sigh:

"You came in here at a quarter past ten, I think you said? That's right, isn't it? How can you be so sure about the time?"

Félicie's lips twitched in a little patronizing smile.

"Come over here," she said.

He went across to her, and she pointed to the room behind the shop, which served as a kitchen for Mélanie Chochoi. In the dim interior could be seen a cane armchair, on which lay a ginger cat rolled up in a ball on a red cushion, and just above it, on a shelf, an alarm clock with the hands standing at ten-seventeen.

Félicie had been right. She always was. As for the little shopkeeper, she was wondering what on earth these people had come for.

"What did you buy?"

"A pound of butter. Give me a pound of butter, please, Madame Chochoi. The Chief Superintendent wishes me to do exactly as I did the day before yesterday. Now then, *demi-sel* next, wasn't it? And then . . . let me think. . . . A package of pepper, a can of tomatoes, and two cutlets . . . Put them in my string bag, will you?"

Everything seemed strange to Maigret that morning. He could not shake off the feeling that he was as out of place in this little world as a giant in a toy village.

A few miles from Paris, he had diverged from the route along the Seine. At Poissy, he had climbed the hill, and then suddenly, surrounded by real fields and orchards, there before him was this isolated little community. Its name, proclaimed a signboard beside the newly built road, was JEANNEVILLE ESTATE.

A few years earlier, this must have been an area of fields, meadows, and thickets, like the surrounding countryside, until the advent of a property developer with a wife or mistress named Jeanne, after whom, no doubt, this embryo village had been named.

Streets had been mapped out, the avenues of the future, and lined with immature trees, their thin trunks packed with straw to protect them from frost.

Here and there, houses and cottages had been built. It was neither a village nor a town, but something different from either. It was unfinished, with gaps between the houses, a great deal of scaffolding, and patches of empty ground, and, in the streets, useless standard gas lamps, an absurd refinement, since the streets could barely be said to exist apart from the blue plaques inscribed with their names.

DREAM HOUSE, WORLD'S END, OPEN HOUSE—every cottage had its name on a board, surrounded by scrollwork, and down there below was Poissy, the silver ribbon of the Seine dotted with real coal barges, and railroad tracks used by real trains. On the plateau beyond could be seen the farms and bell tower of Orgeval.

Here, only the little old shopkeeper, Mélanie Chochoi, seemed real. She had been lured away from a nearby market town by the promise of a fine new shop, to supply the needs of the new housing development.

"Anything else, dear?"

"Let me think. . . . What else did I buy on Monday? Ah! Yes, hairpins."

Mélanie sold everything, from toothbrushes to face powder, from kerosene to postcards.

"I think that was all, wasn't it?"

Maigret noted that neither Peg Leg's cottage nor the approach to it could be seen from the shop.

"My milk!" exclaimed Félicie. "I nearly forgot my milk!"

7

And, in her usual condescending manner, she explained to Maigret:

"I was so confused with all your questions that I forgot to bring my milk jug. . . . Anyway, I had it with me on Monday. . . . Today, I left it behind. It's in the kitchen. . . . A blue jug with white spots . . . You'll find it next to the stove. . . . That's right, isn't it, Madame Chochoi?"

She spoke in the manner of a queen bestowing a great boon upon a lowly subject, while at the same time implying that she, like Caesar's wife, was above suspicion.

She was most insistent that nothing should be overlooked.

"What did we talk about on Monday, Madame Chochoi?"

"I believe you pointed out that my Zouzou must have worms, seeing that he would keep eating his fur."

Zouzou, presumably, was the tomcat which lay dozing on the red cushion in the armchair.

"Let me see. . . . You collected your *Ciné-Journal* and bought a paperback novel for twenty-five sous."

Spread out on the counter was a variety of cheap novels and magazines with garish covers, but Félicie ignored them and shrugged.

"How much do I owe you? Hurry, please, because the Chief Superintendent wants everything done exactly as it was on Monday, and I wasn't in here as long as this."

"Tell me, Madame Chochoi," interposed Maigret, "while we're on the subject of last Monday morning . . . did you, by any chance, happen to hear a car go by while you were serving Mademoiselle Félicie?"

The shopkeeper gazed out at the sunlit street beyond the glass door.

"I don't know. . . . Let me think. . . . Not that we see many cars around here, though one hears them going past on the main road . . . Monday, did you say? . . . I remember seeing

8

a little red car go past the back entrance to the Sébiles' house. . . . But what day that was, I really couldn't say. . . ."

Just to be on the safe side, Maigret wrote in his notebook: *Red car, Sébile.*

And he and Félicie went out into the street again. Félicie, with her coat draped over her shoulders and her sleeves flapping, swayed as she walked.

"This way. I always take the shortcut home."

A narrow pathway with vegetable gardens on either side.

"Did you meet anyone on the way?"

"You'll see in a minute."

And she was right. He did see. As they emerged into another street, the postman, who had just ridden up the hill, passed by on his bicycle and, turning toward them, called out:

"Nothing for you, Mademoiselle Félicie."

She looked at Maigret.

"He saw me here on Monday at this same time, as he does almost every morning."

The path they were on skirted a hideous pale-blue roughcast cottage, surrounded by a tiny garden in which there stood, beneath the hedge, a row of clay animal sculptures. Félicie went through the gate, her trailing coat brushing against a row of gooseberry bushes as she did so.

"Here we are. This, as you see, is the garden. In a minute, you'll see the summerhouse."

It had been a few minutes short of ten o'clock when they had set out from the cottage, using the front door, which opened onto an avenue. In going to the grocer's and back, they had described a more or less complete circle. They walked beside a border of carnations which would shortly be coming into flower, and then past several beds of tender young green lettuce.

"This is where I expected him to be," stated Félicie, pointing to a length of string stretched taut above a shallow

9

trench. "He'd just started pricking out his tomatoes. As you see, this row is half done. When I saw that *he* wasn't here, I assumed he must have gone indoors for a drop of *vin rosé.*"

"Did he drink a lot?"

"Only when he was thirsty . . . As you will see, he always kept a glass standing bottom up on the barrel in the cellar."

The carefully tended garden of a man of modest means, a cottage such as almost anyone in straitened circumstances might dream of building for his retirement. They passed from the sunlit garden into the bluish shade of the adjoining terrace. There was the little summerhouse on the right, furnished with a table, on which stood a half-bottle of brandy and a little glass with a very thick base.

"You saw the bottle and the glass. Now you told me this morning that your employer never drank alcohol, especially that particular kind, except when he had company."

She looked at him defiantly, meeting his eyes with her own clear blue gaze, as if to proclaim emphatically that she had absolutely nothing to hide.

Yet she could not resist retorting:

"He was not my employer."

"I know. . . . You told me. . . ."

Heavens above! People like Félicie really were maddening to have to deal with. What else was it she had said in that shrill voice of hers that so irritated Maigret? Ah, yes. She had said:

"It would be a breach of trust on my part to reveal secrets that concern others besides myself. Some people, no doubt, look upon me as a servant. . . . But the time will come, I daresay, when they will see things in a different light, when they will discover . . ."

"What will they discover?"

"Nothing."

"Are you insinuating that you were Peg Leg's mistress?"

"What do you take me for?"

10

"His daughter, then?" Maigret had ventured to suggest.

"I refuse to answer. One day, perhaps . . ."

This was the cross he had to bear. Félicie! Stubborn as a mule, acid-tongued, full of strange fancies, her sharp-featured face clumsily daubed with powder and rouge, a little servant girl, given to putting on queenly airs in the local dance hall. And, every now and then, that disturbing, fixed gaze, and at other times that odd, fleeting smile, tinged with irony, if not contempt.

"What if he did take a nip by himself? That's no concern of mine."

But old Jules Lapie, nicknamed Peg Leg, had not been alone; Maigret was convinced of it. A man at work in his garden, wearing clogs and a straw hat, does not suddenly put down his tools to go indoors and fetch a bottle of old brandy from the sideboard, and bring it out to the summerhouse to drink it.

At some stage, there must have been another glass on that green-painted garden table. Someone had removed it. Was it Félicie?

"You say you expected to find Lapie at work in the garden. When you saw that he was not there, what did you do?"

"Nothing. I went into the kitchen, lit the gas to heat the milk, and went to the pump to get some water to wash the vegetables."

"And then?"

"I climbed up on the old chair I keep for the purpose and changed the flypaper."

"Still wearing your hat? You always wear a hat to go shopping, don't you?"

"I'm not a slattern."

"When did you take your hat off?"

"When the milk was ready. I went upstairs. . . ."

Everything in the house, to which the old man had given

11

the name Cape Horn, was fresh and new. The pine staircase smelled of varnish. The stairs creaked.

"Go on up. I'll follow you."

She opened the door of her bedroom, with its chintz-covered mattress that served as a couch and its walls covered with photographs of film stars.

"Here we are. I took off my hat. . . . I thought:

"Oh! I forgot to open Monsieur Jules's bedroom window. . . .

"I crossed the landing. . . . I opened the door, and I cried out. . . ."

Maigret, who had refilled his pipe in the garden, was still puffing at it. He was looking down at the polished floor, gazing at the chalk outline of Peg Leg's body as it had been found lying there on Monday morning.

"And the revolver?" he asked.

"There was no revolver. You know very well there wasn't. It was all in the police report. And don't tell me you haven't read it!"

On the mantelpiece stood a scale model of a three-masted schooner, and the walls were covered with pictures, all of sailing ships, for all the world as if the dead man had been a retired seaman. But the head of the local police, who had handled the case in its early stages, had told Maigret of Peg Leg's one extraordinary adventure.

Jules Lapie had never been a seaman, but had been employed as bookkeeper by a firm in Fécamp, a ship chandler, supplier of sails, rope, winches, and all kinds of ships' stores and provisions.

A bachelor, thickset, persnickety almost to the point of mania, a colorless man, with a brother who was a ship's carpenter.

One morning, Jules Lapie, then about forty, went aboard the *Sainte-Thérèse*, a three-masted schooner due to sail that

12

same day for Chile, to oversee the loading of a cargo of phosphates. Lapie's duties were prosaic enough. It was his task to check that nothing was missing from the consignment as ordered, and to receive payment from the captain.

What precisely had gone wrong? The sailors of Fécamp were never backward in making fun of the persnickety bookkeeper who always seemed so ill at ease when compelled by his duties to set foot on board a ship. Drinks were poured and glasses clinked, as was the custom. He was plied with drink, though God knows what manner of drink it was to make him so very, very drunk.

Be that as it may, when, at high tide, the *Sainte-Thérèse* glided out between the piers of the little harbor of that small port in Normandy, Jules Lapie, who everyone believed, or pretended to believe, had gone ashore, was huddled, dead drunk and snoring, in a corner of the hold.

They battened down the hatches. It was not until they had been two days out at sea that they found him. The captain refused to turn back, to deviate from his course, and thus it came about that Lapie, who in those days still had both his legs, found himself aboard a ship bound for Cape Horn.

This episode was to cost him a leg, when he was thrown through a skylight during a fight.

Years later, he was to be killed by a revolver shot, one Monday in spring, having been lured away from his tomato plants, while Félicie was out getting her supplies from Mélanie Chochoi's brand-new grocery.

"Shall we go downstairs?" murmured Maigret, with a sigh.

The house was so peaceful, so pleasant to be in, with its dollhouse cleanliness and its wholesome smells. The dining room, on the right, had been transformed into a mortuary chapel. The Chief Superintendent opened the door a crack.

The shutters were closed, and the room was in darkness except for the thin slivers of light showing through the slats. The coffin was lying on the table, which was covered with a cloth. Beside it was a bowl of holy water, with a sprig of rosemary in it.

Félicie stood waiting for him at the kitchen door.

"In other words, you know nothing, you saw nothing, you haven't the remotest idea who your employer—sorry! Jules Lapie—could possibly have been entertaining during your absence."

She met his glance unwaveringly, but said nothing.

"And you are quite sure that, when you returned, there was only one glass on the garden table?"

"I saw only one. . . . But if you say there were two . . ."

"Did Lapie have many visitors?"

Maigret sat down next to the stove, reflecting that a drink would be most welcome, preferably a glass of that *vin rosé* mentioned by Félicie. He had seen the barrel down there in the cool, dark cellar. The sun was rising higher in the sky, and, in its heat, the morning dew was gradually evaporating.

"He didn't welcome callers."

Quite a character, this fellow, whose whole life must have been turned upside down by that trip around the Horn! On his return to Fécamp, where, in spite of the loss of his leg, his strange adventure was viewed with some mirth, he withdrew still further into himself, and devoted his energy to a prolonged lawsuit against the owners of the *Sainte-Thérèse*. He claimed that, since he had been detained aboard against his will, the shipping company was at fault, and was therefore liable to pay compensation. He set the highest possible value on his amputated leg, won his case, and was awarded substantial damages.

The people of Fécamp thought him a figure of fun. He shunned them and, having come to hate the sea, moved inland,

14

and was one of the first to succumb to the lure of the dazzling prospects held out by the developer of Jeanneville.

He engaged a girl whom he had known as a child in Fécamp to come and keep house for him.

"How long have you lived in this house?"

"Seven years."

"You are now twenty-four . . . so you were seventeen when . . ."

Allowing his thoughts to drift at will, he suddenly asked:

"Have you got a steady boyfriend?"

She looked at him, but did not answer.

"I asked you if you had a steady boyfriend."

"My private life is no concern of yours."

"Does he visit you here?"

"I don't have to answer that."

She deserved a good slap, she really did. It was not the first time that Maigret had been tempted to administer one, or at least to take her by the shoulders and shake her.

"No matter. I'll soon find out."

"You won't find anything out."

"Oh? That's what you think, is it?"

He pulled himself up. It was really too absurd. He was not going to demean himself by having an argument with this chit of a girl.

"Are you sure you have nothing more to tell me? Think it over while there is still time."

"I've done all the thinking that's necessary."

"Sure you're not hiding something from me?"

"If you're as clever as they say, how could I hide anything from you?"

"Well, we'll just have to wait and see."

"I wish you luck."

"What are you planning to do after Jules Lapie's funeral? His family will be coming here, I presume."

15

"I don't know. I hadn't thought."

"Will you be staying here?"

"I might."

"Are you expecting to inherit his property?"

"I think it's very likely."

Maigret did not wholly succeed in controlling his irritation.

"At all events, my dear, I want you to remember one thing. As long as I am investigating this case, I forbid you to leave the area without informing the police."

"Are you putting me under house arrest?"

"No!"

"And what if I should feel like going off somewhere?"

"You will apply to me for permission."

"Do you think I killed him?"

"My thoughts are my own, and I have no intention of sharing them with you."

He had had enough. He was furious, mainly for having allowed himself to get into such a state over a nonentity like Félicie. Twenty-four, was she? It seemed hardly possible. The way she was carrying on, one would take her for a youngster of twelve or thirteen, solemnly playing out some juvenile fantasy or other of her own.

"Good-bye."

"Good-bye."

"Oh, by the way, what are you having for lunch?"

"Don't worry about me. I won't starve."

She could say that again! He could just see her, after he had gone, sitting down at the kitchen table, nibbling at whatever came to hand, and, at the same time, reading one of those paperback romances on sale in Madame Chochoi's shop.

Maigret was still furious. To be made a fool of in front of everyone, and, worse, to be made a fool of by a poisonous little shrew like Félicie!

16

It was Thursday. The Lapie family had turned up in force. There was his brother, Ernest Lapie, the ship's carpenter from Fécamp, an uncouth man with close-cropped, bristling hair and pockmarked face; his wife, a huge woman with a hairy upper lip; and a couple of children she herded along like geese in a field. Then there was a youth of nineteen, a nephew of the dead man, named Jacques Pétillon, who had come from Paris. He seemed nervous and sickly, and was viewed with suspicion by the Lapie contingent.

There was as yet no cemetery in Jeanneville. The procession had set out for Orgeval, of which the new development was a suburb. Félicie created quite a sensation by appearing in a crepe veil. Where on earth could she have got hold of it? Maigret was to learn later that she had borrowed it from Mélanie Chochoi.

Félicie, without waiting to be invited, took her place at the head of the procession. She walked, stiff as a ramrod, in front of the family, the very embodiment of grief, dabbing her eyes with a black-edged handkerchief, also no doubt borrowed from Mélanie, which she had sprayed with cheap eau de Cologne.

Sergeant Lucas, who had spent the night in Jeanneville, was at Maigret's side. Both were walking at the rear of the procession along the dusty road, listening to the larks singing in the clear sky.

"She knows something, that's for sure. She's so sharp, she'll cut herself one of these days. . . ."

Lucas nodded in agreement. The doors of the little church were left open throughout the service, so that the scents of springtime were even more pervasive than the incense. It was not far from the church to the graveside.

After the ceremony, the family were to return to the cottage, to deal with the matter of the will.

"Why did my brother have to make a will?" exclaimed

17

Ernest Lapie in surprise. "We don't go in for that kind of thing in our family."

"According to Félicie . . ."

"Félicie! Félicie! I'm sick of the sound of her name."

Involuntarily, Maigret shrugged.

And there she was, shouldering her way to the front, making sure of being the first to throw a spadeful of earth on the coffin. And having done so, she left the graveside in floods of tears, walking so fast that it seemed she was almost bound to trip and fall.

"Stay with her, Lucas."

She walked and walked at a very brisk pace, taking advantage of the twists and turns of the streets and lanes of Orgeval. Lucas followed, barely fifty yards behind her, but eventually, coming out into a more or less deserted street, he saw the back of a delivery truck disappearing around a corner, and realized that he had lost her.

He went into the nearest café.

"Tell me . . . that truck that's just driven off . . ."

"Yes . . . It belongs to the car mechanic, Louvet. He just looked in for a quick one. . . ."

"Did he give a lift to anyone?"

"I don't know. . . . I don't think so. . . . I didn't see him leave."

"Do you know where he's bound for?"

"Paris. He always goes there on Thursdays."

Lucas hurried over to the post office, which, by a lucky chance, was just across the street.

"Hello . . . Yes . . . Lucas speaking . . . This is urgent. . . . A delivery truck, rather battered . . . Hang on a minute. . . ."

He turned to the postmistress.

"Do you happen to know the license number of Monsieur Louvet's truck?"

18

"No . . . but I do remember that the last figure is an eight."

"Hello . . . The last figure is eight. A young woman dressed in mourning . . . Hello . . . Don't hang up. . . . No, I don't want her arrested. Just followed . . . understand? . . . You'll be hearing further from the Chief Superintendent himself."

He returned to join Maigret, who was walking alone behind the family on the Orgeval-Jeanneville road.

"She got away."

"What do you mean?"

"She must have jumped into the delivery truck as soon as it stopped. . . . By the time I turned the corner, it was too late. I called the Quai des Orfèvres. They're putting out an all-points alert. They're keeping watch on all roads into Paris."

So, Félicie had vanished! Without fuss, in broad daylight, under the very noses of Maigret and his most trusted assistant! She had vanished, in spite of that voluminous mourning veil, which made her conspicuous a mile off.

The family mourners kept looking back at the two policemen, wondering where on earth Félicie could have got to. She had taken the front-door key with her. They had to go in through the garden. Maigret opened the dining-room shutters. The table was still covered with a sheet, the sprig of rosemary had been left lying there, and the whole place smelled of candle grease.

"I could do with a drink," said Ernest Lapie, sighing. "Etienne! Julie! Keep off the flower beds! There must be some wine somewhere."

"In the cellar," Maigret told him.

Lapie's wife had gone to Mélanie's shop to buy some cookies for the children, and, while she was about it, she got enough for everyone.

"My brother had no reason whatsoever to make a will,

19

Chief Superintendent. I realize that he was eccentric. . . . He was unsociable, to say the least, and didn't bother to keep in touch. . . . All the same . . ."

Maigret was rummaging through the drawers of the little desk that stood in a corner of the room. He took out several bundles of bills and receipts neatly fastened together, and there underneath lay an old gray wallet. It contained nothing but a single buff envelope.

To be opened after my death.

"Well, gentlemen, this is what we are looking for, I think."

I, Jules Lapie, the undersigned, being sound in mind and body, do hereby declare, in the presence of Ernest Forrentin and François Lepape, both residing in Jeanneville, in the district of Orgeval . . .

As Maigret read on, his voice took on a graver tone.

"Félicie was right!" he said, when he had finished. "It is she who inherits the house and all its contents."

The relatives were quite simply thunderstruck. The will contained one phrase that they would not readily forget:

Having regard to the attitude that my brother and his wife saw fit to adopt at the time of my accident . . .

"All I said was that I couldn't see the point of moving heaven and earth just because . . ." expostulated Ernest Lapie.

In view of the conduct of my nephew, Jacques Pétillon . . .

The sickly young man from Paris wore the hangdog expression of an undistinguished schoolboy on Prize Day.

All to no avail. Félicie was the heir. And Félicie, for God knows what reason, had vanished.

20

2

In the Métro

Maigret, with his hands in his trouser pockets, stood facing the bamboo coatrack in the entryway, with its lozenge-shaped mirror beneath the pegs. The sight of his face reflected in this mirror might well have brought a smile to his lips, for he was reminded of a shamefaced child longing to gratify an unreasonable whim. Yet Maigret did not smile, but, after some hesitation, stretched out his hand, seized the wide-brimmed straw hat that was hanging from one of the pegs, and put it on his head.

Well, well! Old Peg Leg had had an even bigger head than the Chief Superintendent, who always had difficulty finding a hat large enough to fit him. Deep in thought, still wearing the straw hat, he went into the dining room, to take another look at the photograph of Jules Lapie that he had found in a drawer.

Once, on being asked to comment on Maigret's methods by a visiting criminologist, the Chief Commissioner of the Police Judiciaire had replied, with an enigmatic smile:

"Maigret? How can I put it? He settles into a case as if it were a pair of comfortable old slippers."

Today, it would not have taken much to induce the Chief Superintendent to step not into the victim's slippers so much

21

as into his clogs. For there they stood, inside the door on the right, obviously just where they were supposed to be. There was a place for everything, and everything was in its place. Except for the absence of Félicie, Maigret would have been prepared to believe that life was going on just as usual in the house, that he himself was Lapie, on the point of making his slow way into the garden, to finish pricking out his row of tomatoes.

Behind the freshly painted cottages that could be seen from the garden, the sky was filled with the glorious colors of sunset. Ernest Lapie, the dead man's brother, had sent his family back to Fécamp, announcing that he himself was proposing to spend the night in Poissy. The others, the neighbors and the few farm workers from Orgeval who had attended the funeral, had doubtless returned to their homes, or dropped into the Anneau d'Or, the local inn, for a drink.

Sergeant Lucas was also at the inn, Maigret having instructed him to take his suitcase there, and to stay within reach of the telephone, pending further news from Paris.

Peg Leg had had a huge head, a square jaw, thick gray eyebrows, and gray bristles all over his face, since it was his habit to shave only once a week. He had been mean with money. One only had to glance through his bills. It was obvious that, as far as he was concerned, every penny counted. His brother had admitted:

"To be sure, he was careful. . . ."

And in Normandy, when one man says of another that he is "careful" . . .

It was a mild evening. The sky was visibly changing from rose to violet. Fresh breezes were blowing in from the countryside, and Maigret, his pipe clenched between his teeth, caught himself stooping a little, as Lapie had done. More than that, as he made for the cellar, he found that he was dragging his left leg. He turned on the tap of the barrel of *vin rosé*, rinsed the glass, and helped himself. At this hour, Félicie would normally be at work in the kitchen, and the smell of simmering stew would no doubt be drifting out into the garden. This surely was the time of day for watering the plants. He could see people out with their watering cans in the neighboring gardens. Dusk was spreading through the rooms of Cape Horn, where, no doubt, in the old man's time, the lighting of the lamps was delayed until the last possible moment.

Why had he been killed? Maigret could not help reflecting that he, too, would one day retire to a little house in the country, with a garden, a broad-brimmed straw hat. . . .

Theft could not have been the motive, since, according to his brother, Peg Leg possessed almost nothing apart from the quarterly payment of his famous damages. A savings-bank book had been found in the house, along with an envelope containing two thousand francs, and a few premium bonds. His gold watch had also been found.

Oh, well! They would have to look elsewhere. But first, he would have to dig deeper into the old man's character. He had been grumpy, churlish, taciturn, persnickety. A loner. The smallest disruption of his settled habits must have infuriated him. He had never even entertained the thought of marriage and a family, and, as far as was known, had never had a love affair of any description.

What had Félicie been hinting at? No, really! Félicie was a liar. Lying was as natural to her as breathing. Or, at least, bending the truth to suit herself. Being just a servant to the old man was altogether too humdrum. So she chose to let it be understood that the reason he sent for her to come and live with him . . .

Maigret turned toward the kitchen window. How had they got along together, those two lonely souls, so cut off from the rest of the world? Maigret had a feeling—no, a conviction —that they had fought like cat and dog.

Suddenly . . . Maigret gave a start . . . He had just come

23

from the cellar, having helped himself to a second glass of wine. There he stood, in the dusk, with the straw hat on his head. For a moment, he thought he must be dreaming. A light had been switched on behind the lace curtains in the kitchen, gleaming saucepans sprang into view on glossy painted shelves. The phut of a gas jet could be heard. The Chief Superintendent glanced at his watch. It was ten to eight.

He opened the door, and there was Félicie, who had already taken off her hat and veil and hung them on the coatrack, putting a pan of water on to boil.

"Oh! So you're back!"

She did not seem surprised, but merely looked him up and down, taking in the straw hat, which Maigret had by now forgotten.

He sat down near the window in what must have been the old man's chair, and stretched out his legs. Félicie went about her business as if he were not there. She set the table for her dinner, and fetched butter, bread, and sausage from the cupboard.

"Tell me, my dear . . ."

"I'm not your dear."

"Tell me, Félicie . . ."

"Mademoiselle Félicie, if you don't mind."

Heavens above! Why did she have to be so disagreeable? It was maddening, like trying to get hold of some slithering wild creature, such as a lizard or a grass snake. It bothered him to have to take her seriously, but he felt he had no choice, since it was only through her that he could hope to arrive at the truth.

"I asked you not to leave Jeanneville."

She smiled smugly, as if to say:

"Well, you couldn't stop me, could you? So there!"

"What did you go to Paris for, may I ask?"

"Just for the ride."

24

"Indeed? I may as well tell you that, any time now, I shall be getting a detailed report on where you went and what you did."

"I know. Don't think I didn't see that great oaf you had tail me."

"What great oaf?"

"He was tall, with red hair. I changed trains six times on the Métro, but I couldn't shake him off."

Inspector Janvier, no doubt. He must have got on her track as soon as the mechanic put her down at Porte Maillot.

"Who did you go to see?"

"No one."

She sat down to eat. What is more, she put one of her paperback romances on the table in front of her—she had marked her place with a knife—and settled down for a quiet read.

"Tell me, Félicie."

She had a forehead like a nanny goat's. The Chief Superintendent had been struck by it the very first time he saw her. A high, stubborn forehead, butting away obstinately at anything that stood in its path.

"Do you intend to spend the night alone in this house?"

"What about you? Are you planning to stay?"

She ate, she read. Smothering his exasperation, he looked at her quizzically, and tried to sound as fatherly as he could.

"You told me this morning that you were sure he had made you his heir. . . ."

"Well! What of it?"

"How did you know?"

"I just did, that's all."

She had made coffee, and she now poured herself a cup. She obviously liked her coffee, and she lingered over it, savoring it, but she did not offer any to Maigret.

"I'll come and see you tomorrow."

25

"Suit yourself."

"By then, I hope you will have had time to reconsider."

She looked him boldly in the eye, giving him the full benefit of her clear, inscrutable gaze, shrugged, and murmured:

"What is there to reconsider?"

Outside the front door of Cape Horn, Maigret found Inspector Janvier waiting for him. He had followed his quarry all the way back to Jeanneville. His cigarette glowed in the dark. It was a fine, starlit night. The only sound was the croaking of frogs.

"I knew her at once, Chief, from the description Lucas gave me over the telephone. When the truck drove up to the city gate, the young lady was sitting in front with the driver, all very friendly. Then she got out. She walked up Avenue de la Grande-Armée, looking in the shopwindows. On the corner of Rue Villaret-de-Joyeuse she went into a patisserie, and ate half a dozen cream puffs and drank a glass of port."

"Did she spot you?"

"I don't think so."

"I know she did."

Janvier looked somewhat abashed.

"Next, she went into the Métro. She bought a second-class ticket. She kept moving from one line to another—the trains were almost empty at that hour. She changed first at Place de la Concorde, then at Gare Saint-Lazare. . . . She had a paperback novel in her bag, and she read it between stops. . . . We changed five times in all."

"Did she speak to anyone?"

"No one . . . As time went on, the cars began to fill up. By six o'clock, with all the shops and offices closing, they were jammed tight. . . . You know how it is. . . ."

"Go on."

"At Place des Ternes, we were so jostled by the crowd that

26

we found ourselves almost shoulder to shoulder. I confess it was only then that I realized she knew she was being followed. She looked straight at me. I had the impression, Chief . . . How shall I put it? . . . For a few seconds her face seemed to change completely. It was as if she was afraid. . . . I'm convinced that for those few seconds she was afraid, of me or of something. . . . It was over in a flash, and she was elbowing her way onto the platform."

"Are you sure she didn't speak to anyone?"

"Quite sure. She waited on the platform for the train to come in, and peered into the most crowded car."

"Did she show any particular interest in any of the passengers?"

"I couldn't really tell. What I do know is that she had quite recovered from her momentary panic, and that, as the train disappeared into the darkness of the tunnel, she couldn't resist turning to me with a look of triumph. Then she hurried up the steps to the exit. . . . I don't think she knew quite where she was. . . . She had an apéritif in a bar on the corner of Avenue des Ternes, then consulted a railroad timetable and took a taxi to Gare Saint-Lazare. And that's all. I took the same train as she did to Poissy, and then followed her up the hill on foot."

"Have you had anything to eat?"

"I managed to grab a sandwich at the station."

"Wait here. I'll send Lucas to relieve you."

Maigret set off for Orgeval, leaving Jeanneville to the peace of the night, with just a few windows here and there showing a rosy light. It was not long before he was reunited with Lucas in the Anneau d'Or at Orgeval. Lucas was not alone. His companion, wearing blue coveralls, could be none other than the car mechanic, Louvet. The young man was in a very animated state, which was hardly surprising seeing that he already had four or five saucers piled up in front of him.

27

Lucas also had alcohol on his breath as he made the introductions.

"As I was telling the Sergeant, Chief Superintendent, I hadn't the least inkling when I set off in my jalopy . . . I go to Paris every Thursday afternoon to stock up with spare parts and things."

"Always at the same time of day?"

"More or less."

"Was Félicie aware of that?"

"To tell you the truth, I hardly know her. . . . I've seen her around, but never to talk to. I did know Peg Leg, though, because he came in here every night for his game of cards with Forrentin and Lepape. Sometimes the landlord would make up a fourth, and sometimes I would. . . . As a matter of fact, Forrentin and Lepape are here now, over there in the corner, to the left, with the Mayor and the builder."

"When did you discover you had a passenger?"

"Just before I got to Saint-Germain . . . I heard a sigh behind me. At first I thought it was just the wind, because there was a bit of a breeze, and the tarpaulin was flapping. . . . Then, suddenly, there was this voice, asking me if I had a light. . . . I turned around, and there she was, with her veil thrown back, and a cigarette in her mouth.

"She was in no laughing mood, I can tell you. She was as white as a sheet, and the cigarette shook between her lips.

" 'What on earth are you doing here?' I asked.

"And then it all came pouring out. . . . She said she absolutely had to get to Paris. There was not a moment to lose. It was a matter of life and death. The people who killed Peg Leg were after her, and the police couldn't do a thing about it.

"I stopped the truck for a minute, so that she could get in the front beside me, because she was sitting on an old crate in the back, and it was none too clean. . . .

28

" 'Later . . . later,' she kept repeating. 'When I've done what I have to do, I may tell you the whole story. . . . Anyway, I'll be eternally grateful to you for this. You have saved my life.'

"When we got to the city gate, she thanked me, and got out. Her manner was very grand, as if she was a princess or something."

Lucas and Maigret exchanged glances.

"Now, if it's all the same to you, we'll have one final drink. Oh, yes, I insist. It's my round. And I'll be off and have a bite to eat. This isn't going to get me into any trouble, is it? Cheers!"

Ten o'clock at night. Lucas was mounting guard outside Cape Horn, having relieved Janvier, who had gone back to Paris. The dining room of the Anneau d'Or was blue with smoke. Maigret had eaten too much, and was on his third or fourth drink of the local so-called marc.

Sitting astride a rush-seated chair, with his elbows on the back rail, he seemed at times to fall into a doze, with his eyes half shut and the smoke drifting upward from the bowl of his pipe.

Opposite him were four men playing cards on a table covered with a crimson cloth. Fingering the grubby cards as they talked, they answered questions and told an occasional anecdote. The landlord, Monsieur Joseph, was filling the gap left by old Lapie, and the mechanic, having had his supper, had returned to take the fourth hand.

"To put it in a nutshell," said Maigret, sighing, "he lived like a fighting cock. His social position was not unlike that of a respectable country parson, looked after by a faithful housekeeper. I daresay he wasn't averse to a bit of cosseting, and . . ."

Lepape, who was deputy mayor of Orgeval, winked at the others. His partner, Forrentin, was manager of the new development, and lived in the best house, overlooking the main road, not far from the billboard advertising the remaining plots for sale in Jeanneville.

"A parson and his housekeeper, that's rich!" sniggered the Deputy Mayor.

Forrentin contented himself with a sarcastic smile.

"Oh, come! You didn't know him. Anyone can see that," exclaimed the landlord, having called a run of three and *belote*. "Even though he's dead, there's no denying he was as pig-headed as they come."

"In what way?"

"Well, for one thing, he moaned and groaned from morning to night, about anything and everything. He was never satisfied. . . . Well! Take that business over the glasses. . . ."

He appealed to the others for confirmation.

"First, he complained that my liqueur glasses were too thick, and he went and rummaged on my shelves till he found an odd one right at the back that suited him. Then, one day, by pouring his drink from his own glass into one of the others, he found that they held exactly the same amount, and he was furious.

" 'Well, seeing you chose that particular glass yourself!' I protested.

"And the upshot was that he went into town and bought another glass, and brought it to me. And that one held nearly half as much again as mine did.

" 'I don't mind,' I said, 'so long as you pay me an extra twenty-five centimes.'

"After that, I didn't set eyes on him again for a whole week. Then one evening, there he was, standing in the doorway.

" 'Will you fill my glass?'

" 'For an extra twenty-five centimes,' I repeated.

"So he went away again. This went on for a whole month,

30

and I was the one who had to give way in the end, because we needed him to make a fourth at cards.

"Doesn't that prove my point, that he was as pigheaded as they come? And he was the same with his servant girl. They were at loggerheads from morning to night. You could hear them at it for miles. Then one of them would sulk, and it would go on for weeks at a time. In the long run, though, I think she got the better of him, because, saving your presence, she's even more pigheaded than he was. Still, I would like to know who killed the poor fellow. He wasn't a bad man, at heart. . . . It was just the way he was made. He never played a hand at cards without complaining, at some point, that someone was cheating."

A little while later, Maigret asked:

"Did he often go to Paris?"

"Practically never. Just once a quarter, to collect his compensation. He used to go there and back in a day."

"And Félicie?"

"Say, fellows, do any of you know whether Félicie ever went to Paris?"

They had no information on this point. On the other hand, they knew that she often went dancing on Sunday at a dance hall on the waterfront at Poissy.

"Do you know what the old man called her? He always referred to her as his 'Poll Parrot,' because of the peculiar clothes she wears. You see, Chief Superintendent—this won't please my good friend Forrentin, but I speak as I find—everybody who lives in Jeanneville is more or less crazy. It's not a real community. It's full of poor devils who have scrimped and saved all their lives to buy a little place in the country for their retirement. Well, when the day comes, they fall for Forrentin's glowing sales talk. . . . Don't attempt to deny it, Forrentin. You know very well you're a wizard at gilding the pill. . . . So there they are at last in their earthly paradise, and it doesn't take

31

them long to find out that all they have bought is damned boredom at a hundred francs an hour. . . .

"Only, by then it's too late. They've invested the whole of their miserable pittance in the place, and they have to find their fun where they can get it, or manufacture it as best they can. . . . One will go to law over the branch of a tree overhanging his garden, another because some dog has cocked its leg against his begonias . . . and some . . ."

Maigret was not asleep, and, to prove it, he stretched out his arm for his glass and raised it to his lips. But the heat had made him drowsy, and he allowed his thoughts to drift back gently to Jeanneville. Bit by bit, he reconstructed it in his mind, its unfinished avenues, its infant trees, its houses, seemingly built of toy bricks, its tiny, carefully tended gardens, its clay animals and glass witch balls.

"Did he never have any visitors?"

It didn't make sense. Such a quiet, uneventful, self-contained existence. If there had really been no more to his life than that, surely it was inconceivable that one morning, only last Monday, in fact, while Félicie was out doing her shopping at Mélanie Chochoi's grocery store, Peg Leg should suddenly have been impelled to abandon his tomato plants, go to the sideboard in the dining room, get out the bottle of brandy and a glass, and then sit all by himself in the summerhouse, sipping the brandy normally reserved for very special occasions. And, after that . . .

He had been wearing his gardening hat when he went upstairs to his bedroom, with its highly polished floor. What had he gone there for?

No one had heard the shot, and yet a revolver had been fired by someone, at point-blank range, someone who, according to the ballistics report, had been standing less than two feet away from the old man.

At least if the revolver had been found, it might have

been supposed that Peg Leg had gone out of his mind and . . .

The Deputy Mayor, adding up his score, was troubled by no such doubts. He murmured, as if it explained everything:

"What is there to say? He was an eccentric."

Very true. But he was dead. Someone had killed him. And Félicie, looking as if butter wouldn't melt in her mouth, as usual, had given the police the slip right after the funeral, and hitched a lift to Paris, where she had gazed in the shopwindows, just as if nothing had happened, and eaten cream puffs, had a glass of port, and, to crown it all, gone for a joy ride on the Métro!

"I wonder who'll get the house?"

The cardplayers chatted intermittently. To Maigret, who was not listening, their voices provided a background murmur to his thoughts. He did not tell them that the house now belonged to Félicie. He was drifting. Impressions formed and dissolved. He had lost all sense of time and place. Félicie, by now, was probably in bed, reading. Being left all alone in the house where her employer had been murdered did not seem to worry her. . . . Ernest Lapie, the dead man's brother, chagrined by the terms of the will . . . He was not short of money, but it was beyond him why his brother . . .

"It's a well-built house. The best in the development."

Who had said that? Forrentin, probably.

"And what's more, it's got charm. It's a convenient size, too, spacious and yet compact."

Maigret recalled the gleaming staircase. Whatever might be said of Félicie, no one could deny that she kept the place spotlessly clean. As Maigret's mother used to say, you could eat off the floor.

A door on the right . . . the old man's bedroom . . . A door on the left . . . Félicie's . . . Adjoining Félicie's bedroom, another room, much larger, crammed with furniture.

33

Maigret frowned. You couldn't call it a presentiment, still less an idea. It was no more than a vague feeling that there was something not quite right about the setup.

"In the young man's time . . ." Lepape remarked.

Maigret started.

"The nephew, do you mean?"

"Yes. He lived with his uncle for six months or more. . . . It must have been about a year ago. . . . He was in poor health. Apparently it was thought that a spell in the country might do him good, after living in Paris all that time."

"Where did he sleep?"

"Ah! There you have it. . . . It's sort of a joke, really."

Lepape winked. Forrentin looked disapproving. It was plain to see that the manager frowned on gossip concerning the development over which, in his own estimation, he held absolute dominion.

"That doesn't mean a thing," he protested.

"Well, was there or was there not anything between the old man and Félicie? See here, Chief Superintendent, you know the layout of the house. Upstairs on the right, there is one bedroom, the one occupied by Peg Leg. On the opposite side there are two rooms, but you have to go through the first one to get to the second. Well, when the young man moved in, his uncle put him in his own bedroom, and moved in across the way. In other words, to all intents and purposes, he moved in with Félicie. He slept in the first room, and she moved into the one beyond, which meant that to get to and from her own bedroom she had to go through the old man's. . . ."

Forrentin was affronted.

"Would it have been preferable, do you think, to put an eighteen-year-old youth in with the girl?"

"Not at all, not at all," protested Lepape, looking sly. "I'm not making any insinuations. All I'm saying is that the old man was sleeping next door to Félicie, while the nephew was well

34

out of the way across the landing. As to any suggestion that there was something funny going on . . ."

Maigret, for his part, was not thinking along these lines. Not that he had any illusions about the proclivities of elderly or even quite old men. And besides, Peg Leg was only sixty, and a vigorous sixty at that.

It was just that the notion did not fit in with the view he personally had formed of the man. He felt he was beginning to understand this cross-grained recluse, whose hat he had recently worn.

Whatever it was that was worrying him, it was not the old man's relationship with Félicie. What was it, then? It had something to do with the layout of the rooms.

He repeated to himself, like a schoolboy memorizing a lesson:

"The nephew on the right . . . all alone . . . the uncle on the left, and then Félicie . . ."

So the uncle had interposed himself between the two of them. Had he wanted to prevent the young people from getting together behind his back? Had his idea been to keep Félicie on a tight rein? No, because as soon as his nephew left the house, he had returned to his former quarters, and left her to her own devices on the other side of the landing.

"Let it rest for tonight, Chief."

He stood up. He was going upstairs to bed. He could hardly wait for tomorrow, when he would return to the toy village and once more see the little brick cottages, rosy in the sunlight, and take another look at those three bedrooms. But first, he would put a call through to Janvier in Paris, to tell him to find out all he could about the young man.

Up to now, Maigret had scarcely given him a thought. No one had seen him in Jeanneville on the morning of the murder. He was a tall, thin youth, high-strung, unlikely to do much good, but Maigret could not see him committing a murder.

According to report, his mother, Lapie's sister, had married a violinist, who used to perform in cheap local restaurants. He had died young. In order to support her son, she had taken a job as cashier with a textile firm on Rue du Sentier, and she, in her turn, had died, two years ago.

A few months after her death, Lapie had taken the young man into his home. They had not seen eye to eye, which was not surprising. Jacques Pétillon was a musician, like his father before him, and Peg Leg was not the man to put up with the scraping of a violin or the blaring of a saxophone in his house.

Now, Jacques Pétillon earned his living as a saxophone player in a nightclub on Rue Pigalle. He lived in a furnished room on the sixth floor of a boardinghouse on Rue Lepic.

Maigret sank into the soft feather mattress on his bed and fell asleep, with mice scampering about all night above his head. The room had a wholesome country smell, a compound of hay and mildew, and in the morning he awoke to the lowing of cows, and the wheezing of the local bus as it approached the Anneau d'Or. Then he breathed in the aroma of coffee laced with brandy.

About those bedrooms . . . But first he must telephone Janvier.

"Hello . . . The address is the Hotel Beauséjour, Rue Lepic. . . . Good hunting, old boy."

And he lumbered off to Jeanneville, whose rooftops seemed to grow out of an undulating sea of oats. As he ambled along, a very odd thing happened. He quickened his pace and peered ahead, eager for his first sight of the windows of Cape Horn, and for . . . Well, yes! It must be admitted. Eager for his first sight of Félicie. He could picture her already at work in her kitchen, with her sharp features and her nanny-goat forehead, receiving him as rudely as she knew how, and gazing at him out of her clear, inscrutable eyes.

Was he already beginning to miss her?

36

He understood, he guessed, he was certain that **Peg Leg** had needed this dear enemy as much as he had needed his glass of wine from the barrel, the air he breathed, his nightly game of cards, and his squabbles with his partners over a run of three or a trump.

In the distance, he could see Lucas stamping up and down in the lane. It must have been a chilly night for him, keeping watch out there. And then, through the open window of her bedroom, he saw tendrils of dark hair escaping from a turban of sorts, then a tense figure shaking out bedding. He had been seen. He had been recognized. Doubtless, the question of how he should be received was already being considered.

In spite of himself, he smiled. Félicie was there, all right!

3

The Diary

"Hello! Is that you, Chief? . . . Janvier speaking . . ."

The day was oppressive. It was not just that there was thunder in the air, or that, every now and then, Maigret had to wipe a thin film of perspiration from his face, or that his fingers were twitching with impatience. It reminded him a little of the distress he used to feel as a child when he happened to be where he ought not to have been and knew perfectly well that he was wanted elsewhere.

"Where are you calling from?"

"Rue des Blancs-Manteaux. I'm speaking from a small watchmaker's shop. . . . Our friend is all alone in a filthy bistro opposite. He seems to be waiting for something or someone. He's just had another glass of brandy."

A pause. Maigret knew very well what the Inspector was going to say next.

"I was wondering, Chief . . . don't you think you'd better come yourself and . . . ?"

The pressure had been on him since early that morning, but Maigret had stubbornly continued to resist it.

"Carry on the good work. Call me if there are any new developments."

Was he doing the right thing, he wondered. Was this

really the proper way to go about things? And yet he could not bring himself to leave Jeanneville. Something was holding him back, though just what it was, he could not say.

A very odd case this was turning out to be. Fortunately for him, the press had shown no interest in Peg Leg's death. At least twenty times he had caught himself muttering under his breath:

"And yet the old man *was* murdered."

It was as if the murder was somehow of secondary importance, as if, in spite of himself, he was obsessed with quite a different problem. And that problem, needless to say, was Félicie.

The landlord of the Anneau d'Or had lent him an old bicycle. Astride it, Maigret looked like a performing bear. But it enabled him to go back and forth between Orgeval and the housing development as often as he pleased.

The weather was still glorious. Spring and sunshine would always be associated in his mind with this locality. Flowers growing all along the low garden walls, and in the beds and borders. Retired people whose hobby was gardening turning their heads indolently to watch the Chief Superintendent or Sergeant Lucas go by, for Maigret had decided to keep Lucas with him.

Lucas also was of the opinion that this was an odd way of going about things, but he kept his thoughts to himself. He was fed up with pacing up and down outside Cape Horn. What was he supposed to be doing there, anyway? Keeping an eye on Félicie? All the windows in the house were open. The girl could be plainly seen going about her business. She had gone out to do her shopping as usual. She knew that she was being followed. Was it thought that she might try to slip away again?

Lucas was puzzled, but he dared not say anything to Maigret. He just champed at the bit, smoked his pipe endlessly, and occasionally relieved his feelings by kicking a pebble.

And yet, since early this morning, it had seemed that the center of interest had shifted away from Jeanneville. The first phone call had come from Rue Lepic. Maigret had been waiting for it, seated on the terrace of the inn, beside a bay tree in a green-painted tub.

He had already established a routine, as he always did, wherever he happened to be. He had an arrangement with the postmistress that she would give him a shout from the window as soon as any call came through from Paris.

"Is that you, Chief? . . . Janvier speaking . . . I'm calling from a café on the corner of Rue Lepic. . . ."

Maigret could see it all: the steep little street, the push-carts piled high with fruit and vegetables, the housewives in their down-at-heel slippers, the colorful hubbub of Place Blanche, and, wedged between two small shops, the Hotel Beauséjour, which he had had occasion to visit in the course of duty more than once in the past.

"Jacques Pétillon didn't get home until six o'clock this morning. He was exhausted. He threw himself on his bed fully dressed. I went to the Pélican, the dive where he works. He hadn't been there all night. What shall I do?"

"Stay where you are. . . . If he goes out, follow him."

Could it be that the nephew was less innocent than he seemed? In any case, Maigret would surely do better to give serious consideration to him instead of concentrating on Félicie. It was plain that this was Janvier's opinion. In the course of his second telephone call, he ventured to hint as much.

"Hello! Janvier speaking . . . The young man has just gone into the tobacconist's on Rue Fontaine. He's as white as a sheet, and he seems very jumpy and uneasy. . . . He keeps looking around, as if he suspected he was being followed, but I don't think he's spotted me. . . ."

So, Pétillon, after snatching a few brief hours of sleep, was on the move again. The tobacconist's shop on Rue Fontaine was the haunt of some pretty unsavory characters.

"What's he doing?"

"He hasn't spoken to anyone. . . . He's watching the door. . . . It looks as if he's waiting for someone. . . ."

"Keep at it. . . ."

In the meantime, Maigret had learned a few more facts about old Lapie's nephew. Why was it that he could not seem to work up an interest in this boy, whose ambition it was to become a famous soloist, and who barely managed to scrape a living by playing the saxophone in a nightclub in Montmartre?

Pétillon had been through some hard times. More than once, he had been forced to take on casual night work as a vegetable porter in Les Halles. Often, he had had to go hungry. And, several times, he had been reduced to pawning his violin.

"Don't you think it's odd, Chief, that he should have been out the whole night, and not set foot in the Pélican, and that now . . . ? I wish you could see him. . . . You ought to see him. . . . He's in torment. He's terrified. You can feel it. . . . Maybe if you could get here . . ."

But Maigret's answer was always the same:

"Keep at it!"

Maigret, in the meantime, perched on his bicycle, plied to and fro between the terrace of the Anneau d'Or, where he sat waiting for phone calls, and Félicie's blue cottage.

He wandered about the place as if he owned it. Félicie went on with her housework, pretending to ignore him. She cooked her meal, having bought what she needed in the morning at Mélanie Chochoi's shop. Sometimes her eyes would meet those of the Chief Superintendent, but he still found it impossible to tell what her feelings were.

As Maigret saw it, she was the one who ought to be afraid. She had been altogether too sure of herself, right from the start. Unless she had something to hide, her attitude simply didn't make sense, and he was watching for the first cracks to appear.

"And yet, the old man *was* murdered."

He could not get her out of his mind. She held the vital clue, and he was determined to wrest it from her. He roamed around the garden. Five or six times he went to the cellar and helped himself to a glass of *vin rosé*. This, too, had become a part of his routine. He had made a discovery. Poking about with a fork in the compost heap near the hedge, he had unearthed a liqueur glass similar to the one he had seen that first day on the table in the summerhouse. He had shown it to Félicie.

"All you have to do is have it tested for fingerprints," she had remarked contemptuously, as if it were no concern of hers.

When he went upstairs to the bedrooms, she did not follow him. He made a thorough search of Lapie's room, and then crossed the landing and began looking through Félicie's drawers. No doubt she could hear him moving about from downstairs. Was she at all apprehensive?

The weather was still perfect, very mild, with a gentle, sweet-scented breeze and bird song coming in through the windows.

Presently, searching through an untidy jumble of stockings and underclothes at the bottom of Félicie's wardrobe, he came upon a diary. He could see why Peg Leg had called her his Poll Parrot. Even her underclothes were in garish colors, shocking pink and acid green, with six-inch insertions of imitation lace.

Hoping by so doing to provoke her, Maigret went down to the kitchen with the diary in his hand. It was dated the previous year. Félicie was engaged in peeling potatoes into a blue enamel basin.

"*13 January.* Why doesn't he come?

"*15 January.* Implored him.

"19 January. Tortured by uncertainty. Is it his wife?

"20 January. Misery.

"23 January. At last!

"24 January. Bliss!

"25 January. More bliss!

"26 January. Him again. His lips, heaven!

"27 January. Life is unfair.

"29 January. Oh, to escape—to escape!"

Every now and then, Maigret looked up from his reading, but Félicie pretended to ignore him.

Maigret affected to laugh. It was a laugh that sounded false in his ears and made him feel like a hotel guest fumbling with the chambermaid and covering it up with a lewd jest.

"What's his name?"

"It's none of your business."

"Married, is he?"

A savage look, like a cat defending its kittens.

"The grand passion, was it?"

She did not reply, but he kept on, feeling ashamed of himself for his persistence. He told himself that it was wrong. He thought of Rue Lepic and Rue Fontaine, and the terrified young man who, ever since last night, had been scurrying hither and thither.

"Now then, my dear, you may as well tell me. Did this man come to visit you here?"

"Why shouldn't he?"

"Was your employer aware of it?"

No! He had had enough of this. The girl was making a fool of him. Not that he expected to fare much better with Mélanie Chochoi, but still, she was next on his list. He propped his bicycle against the front of the shop and waited until Mélanie had finished serving a woman who wanted a can of peas.

"By the way, Madame Chochoi, do you happen to know if Monsieur Lapie's housekeeper had many men friends?"

"I suppose so."

"What do you mean by that?"

"Well, she told me so at any rate. . . . And there was one in particular. . . . But it's not really my business, is it? She seemed very unhappy a lot of the time, poor girl. . . ."

"Was he a married man?"

"Very likely . . . She was always hinting at obstacles. . . . She didn't tell me much, really. . . . If she confided in anyone, it would have been Monsieur Forrentin's maid, Léontine."

A man had been murdered, and here was Maigret, a mature, serious-minded man, concerning himself with the love life of a silly, romantic girl! How foolishly romantic, the entries in her diary showed all too plainly.

"17 June. Misery.

"18 June. Feeling very blue.

"21 June. Happiness is a delusion. There is not enough in the world to go around.

"22 June. I love him.

"23 June. I love him."

Maigret went to Forrentin's house and rang the doorbell. The development manager's maid, Léontine, was a moon-faced girl in her twenties. She was scared at the very sight of him. The last thing she wanted was to get her friend into trouble.

"Of course, she always told me everything. Everything she wanted to tell me, that is . . . She often stopped by to see me, just for a quick visit. . . ."

He could see the two of them so clearly, Léontine with her mouth hanging open in wonder, and Félicie with her coat draped negligently over her shoulders.

"Are you alone? If only you knew."

She would talk and talk, as girls do among themselves.

"I've seen him. . . . I'm so happy."

Poor Léontine was thrown into confusion by Maigret's questions.

"I won't say a thing against her. . . . Félicie has suffered so much!"

"On account of a man?"

"Several times she threatened to kill herself."

"Didn't he return her affection?"

"I don't know. . . . Please don't badger me."

"Do you know his name?"

"She never told me."

"Did you ever see him?"

"No."

"Where did they meet?"

"I don't know."

"Was she his mistress?"

Léontine blushed, and stammered:

"She did say, once, that if she ever had a child . . . What has all this got to do with the old man being murdered?"

Maigret kept going, but he was more and more conscious of a vague, unhappy feeling that he had blundered.

Oh, what the hell! Here he was back on the terrace of the Anneau d'Or. The postmistress called out to him:

"There have been two calls for you from Paris already. I'm expecting them to call back again any minute."

Janvier again. But no, it was not his voice. It was a voice the Chief Superintendent did not recognize.

"Hello! Is that Monsieur Maigret?"

So it could not be anyone from the Quai des Orfèvres.

"I'm a waiter in the buffet at the Gare Saint-Lazare. . . . I'm calling on behalf of a gentleman who asked me to tell you . . . Wait a minute. . . . His name escapes me. . . . It was the name of a month . . . Février . . ."

45

"Janvier."

"That's it. . . . He's on his way by train to Rouen. He couldn't wait to speak to you himself. . . . He wondered whether you could possibly meet his train at Rouen. He said if you were to hire a car . . ."

"Any other message?"

"No, sir. I've told you what he said. There wasn't anything else."

It could mean only one thing. If Janvier has decided on the spur of the moment to take the train to Rouen, it must be because Pétillon is on it. Hastily emerging from the telephone booth, which was stifling, he mopped his face and stood as if uncertain what to do next, under the inquisitive eyes of the postmistress. A car . . . He might manage to get hold of one. . . .

"No, damn it all," he grumbled. "Janvier can figure it out for himself."

Searching the three bedrooms had yielded nothing, apart from Félicie's diary. Poor Lucas, bored and disgusted, was still kicking his heels outside Cape Horn, peered at by the neighbors behind their net curtains.

Instead of rushing off to track down the mysterious nephew, Maigret sat down to a meal on the terrace of the inn, sipped his coffee, washed it down with a glass of old brandy, and then, with a sigh, remounted his bicycle. He stopped at the cottage to slip Lucas a package of sandwiches, and then rode down the hill to Poissy.

It did not take him long to locate the dance hall where Félicie spent most of her free Sundays. It was a wooden building overlooking the Seine. At this time of day it was deserted, and it was the proprietor himself, an Indian in a sweater, who came out to ask him his business. Five minutes later, seated at a table over a couple of drinks, the two men realized that they had met before. It was a familiar experience for Maigret. The

man who now made his living by running a Sunday dance hall
had formerly been a fairground wrestler, and had got into
trouble with the police. He recognized the Chief Superintendent first.

"You're not here on my account, I trust. As you can see,
it's all open and aboveboard here."

"I don't doubt it," said Maigret, with a smile.

"As for the customers . . . No, Chief Superintendent, I
doubt if you'll find anything to interest you here. . . . Salesgirls,
housemaids, decent young boys . . ."

"Do you know a girl named Félicie?"

"Who's she?"

"An odd sort of girl, thin as a stick, with a pointed nose
and a forehead like a nanny goat's, always decked out in all the
colors of the rainbow, like a ship dressed for a review . . ."

"You mean the Parakeet!"

Well, of course. Lapie's name for Félicie had been Poll
Parrot.

"What has she done?"

"Nothing . . . I just wanted to know about the people she
came into contact with here."

"I can't think of anyone really. My wife . . . No, you won't
ever have heard of her; she's on the level. . . . My wife, as I
was saying, called her the Princess, on account of her la-di-da
airs and ways. Who exactly is she, anyway? I never could find
out. . . . She really did carry on as if she was royalty. When she
danced, she held herself as stiff as a poker. When she was asked
about herself, she let it be understood that she was not what
she seemed, but that she wished to remain incognito. A load
of crap, in other words . . . Come to think of it, she always sat
at this table, all by herself. She always sipped her drink with
her little finger stuck out. . . . Her ladyship wouldn't dream of
dancing with just anybody who . . . Last Sunday . . . Bless my
soul! I've just remembered. . . ."

47

Maigret could picture the crowded dance floor and the bouncing wooden planks, the loud strains of the accordion, and the proprietor standing with his hands on his hips, waiting to go around the tables collecting the money.

"She danced with a fellow I'd seen somewhere before, though I can't for the life of me remember where. . . . He was short and thickset, with a crooked nose. . . . But that's not the point. . . . What I did notice was that he held her very close. Then suddenly, right there in the middle of the dance floor, she slapped his face. I thought there was going to be trouble, and I was going to intervene. But not at all. The fellow just slunk off without a word of protest, and her ladyship, all high and mighty, returned to her seat and proceeded to powder her nose. . . ."

By now, Janvier must have been in Rouen for some hours. Maigret propped his bicycle against the terrace of the Anneau d'Or and went across the road to speak to the postmistress. It was refreshingly cool in there.

"Any calls for me?"

"Just one message, asking you to call Police Headquarters in Rouen. Shall I get them for you?"

It was not Janvier who answered, but one of the local inspectors.

"Chief Superintendent Maigret? I have a message for you. The young man, after wandering in and out of a dozen or so bars in Montmartre, took the train to Rouen. Apparently, he spoke to no one, although he seemed to be looking for someone wherever he went. When he got to Rouen, he made straight for the Barracks. He went into a brasserie nearby, a place frequented by prostitutes. . . . I daresay you know of it, the Tivoli. . . . He stayed there about half an hour, then wandered about for a while, and finally ended up at the station. He seemed more and more worn out and discouraged. . . . At present, he's waiting for the train to Paris, and Inspector Janvier is still tailing him."

Maigret gave the usual instructions: the proprietress of the brasserie was to be questioned as to which particular girl Pétillon had come to see, what his business with her had been, and so forth. . . . While he was still in the telephone booth, he heard a rumbling sound, which he took to be a passing bus, but which he realized, when he came out, was distant thunder.

"Are you expecting any more calls?" asked the postmistress, who had never experienced such hustle and bustle in all her uneventful life.

"Very possibly. My sergeant will be taking over for me."

"How fascinating police work must be! We've never seen anything like it, in this quiet little backwater of ours."

He smiled absently, suppressing the temptation to shrug his shoulders, and was soon back once more on the unfinished road leading to the development.

"Sooner or later she'll talk; she must!" he repeated to himself along the way.

There was a storm brewing. Menacing purple clouds were massing on the horizon, the slanting sunbeams seemed to have narrowed, and the atmosphere was oppressive.

"Go back to the Anneau d'Or, Lucas, and wait there in case there are any telephone messages. . . ."

His expression, as he opened the door of Cape Horn, was resolute. He had been put upon long enough. He had reached his limit! He was going to confront that miserable girl once and for all and, if necessary, shake her until her eyes popped out of her head.

"This is it, my dear! Playtime is over!"

She was there all right. He knew she was. He had seen the ground-floor curtain twitch while he was giving Lucas his instructions. He went in. Silence. In the kitchen, a pot of coffee was percolating. In the garden, no one. He frowned.

49

"Félicie," he called softly. "Félicie."

Then angrily, on a rising note, he shouted:

"Félicie!"

For an instant, he was almost persuaded that she had got the better of him again, and slipped through his fingers a second time. But no, he could hear a faint sound upstairs, not unlike the cry of a tiny baby. He took the stairs two at a time and came to a halt in the doorway of Félicie's bedroom when he saw her lying full-length on her couch.

She was crying, with her face buried in the pillow, and at that same moment big raindrops began to fall, and a door, somewhere in the house, was slammed shut by a sudden gust of wind.

"What's the matter?" he growled.

She did not move. Her back shook with sobs. He touched her on the shoulder.

"What's wrong, child?"

"Leave me alone. . . . For God's sake, leave me alone!"

It crossed his mind that this was all just an act, that Félicie had picked her moment, and even arranged herself in this touching attitude, with her dress artfully hitched up well above her bony knees. But he dismissed the thought.

"Get up, my dear."

Well, well! She was actually doing as she was told. The last thing he expected from Félicie was meek, unprotesting obedience. And here she was, sitting on the edge of the couch, her eyes brimming with tears, her face streaked with rouge, gazing at him with such a miserable, weary expression that it made him feel like an absolute brute.

"What's the matter? Come on, now. Tell me all about it."

She shook her head. She was incapable of speech. She made him understand that she would be only too willing to talk if only she could, and then, once more, buried her face in her hands.

50

Standing looming over her in this small room, he felt disproportionately massive, so he drew up a chair, sat down at the foot of her couch, and considered taking hold of her hands and pulling them away from her tear-stained face. For he did not yet quite trust her. It would not altogether have surprised him to discover that, behind those nervously cupped hands, she was smiling sarcastically.

But her tears were genuine. She was crying like a child, unmindful of the ravages to her face. And when at last she spoke, she sounded like a child as well:

"Why are you so horrid to me?"

"Me, horrid? Not at all, child . . . Take it easy, now. Don't you see that I only want what's best for you?"

She shook her head.

"Heavens above! Can't you realize that a murder has been committed, and that you are the only person familiar enough with the ways of this house to . . . I'm not for a moment suggesting that you killed your employer. . . ."

"He wasn't my employer!"

"I know. You told me. . . . Let's say your father, then. . . . Because that's what you've been hinting at all along, isn't it? Very well, let us suppose that old Lapie committed an indiscretion years ago, and later made up for it by taking you into his home. . . . You are his sole heir. . . . You are the only one to benefit from his death."

He was forcing the pace too much. She sprang to her feet and stood straight and stiff as a ramrod, the very embodiment of righteous indignation.

"But it is so, child. Come on now, sit down. On the face of it, you ought to be under arrest."

"I'm quite ready."

Good God! How impossible she was! Maigret would have been happier with the most hardened of hardened criminals, the most intransigent of recidivists. How could one possibly tell

51

when she was playacting and when she was genuine? Was she ever wholly genuine? Even now he could feel that she was watching him the whole time, watching him with quite terrifying penetration.

"That's beside the point. What we need is your help. The man who took advantage of your absence to kill your employer —sorry, to kill Jules Lapie, I mean—must have known enough about your household routine to . . ."

Wearily, she had sat down again on the edge of the couch. She murmured:

"I'm listening."

"And besides, Lapie would never have taken a complete stranger up to his bedroom. . . . He was killed in his bedroom. . . . What could he possibly have been doing there at that hour of the morning? He was working in his garden. He had offered a drink to his visitor, in spite of his known stinginess in such matters. . . ."

Every now and then Maigret almost had to shout to be heard above the noise of the thunder. Then, after an especially loud clap, she put out her hand instinctively, and grasped him by the wrist.

"I'm scared."

She was trembling. She really was trembling.

"You have nothing to fear. I'm here."

What an idiotic thing to say! He realized it almost before the words were out of his mouth. Quick to sense his sympathy, she took full advantage of it, assumed a piteous expression, and bleated:

"You have hurt me so! And now you're going to hurt me again. I'm so unhappy. . . . Dear God! How miserable I am! . . . And you . . . you . . ."

She gazed at him in wide-eyed supplication.

"You keep picking on me because I'm a weak, defenseless girl with no one to protect me. . . . You've had a man out there

52

all night and all day, and he'll be back again tonight."

"What is the name of the man whose face you slapped at the dance hall last Sunday?"

For an instant she looked put out, then she sniggered.

"You see!"

"What's that supposed to mean?"

"It's always me. . . . You bully me and bully me, as if . . . as if you hated me. . . . What have I ever done to you? Yes, I beg you, tell me what harm I have ever done to you?"

At this point Maigret ought to have stood up, asserted himself, and put an end to all this nonsense once and for all. He had had every intention of doing so, thankful at least that there were no witnesses to this absurd scene. But he missed his chance. He was half out of his chair when another roll of thunder gave Félicie an excuse for a fresh outburst of hysteria. She threw herself into his arms and, with her face so close to his that he could feel her hot breath on his cheek, she cried:

"Is it because I'm a woman? Are you another of those men like Forrentin?"

"What's wrong with Forrentin?"

"He wants me. . . . He pesters me. . . . He says that sooner or later he will have his way, and that, in the end, I . . ."

There might be some truth in it. Maigret recalled the manager's face, his furtive smile, his coarse, sensual hands.

"If that's what you want, say so! I'd rather that than . . ."

"No, child, no."

This time he did manage to get to his feet. He pushed her away from him.

"Let's go downstairs, shall we? There's no point in staying up here."

"You came of your own accord. . . ."

"That doesn't mean that I have to stay, still less that I have any ill intentions such as you suggest. . . . Come on, let's go."

53

"Just give me time to tidy up."

She went over to the mirror and dabbed her face with powder, sniveling.

"Something terrible is going to happen—I can feel it—and it will be all your fault!"

"What, for instance?"

"I don't know. . . . But I warn you, if they find me dead . . ."

"Don't be so silly. . . . Come along. . . ."

He made her lead the way. The sky was so overcast that he had to switch on the kitchen light. The coffee was simmering on the stove.

"I think I'd be better off away from here," declared Félicie, turning off the gas.

"Where would you go?"

"Anywhere . . . I don't know. . . . Yes, I'll go right away, somewhere where no one will ever find me. . . . I ought never to have come back."

"You'll stay here."

She muttered something between clenched teeth. He was not sure that he had heard her correctly, but he fancied that what she had said was:

"We'll see about that!"

Taking a shot at random, he said:

"If you're thinking of joining young Pétillon, I'd better tell you right away that he is at this moment in Rouen, in a brasserie frequented by prostitutes."

"It's not . . ."

Then, changing her tack:

"What's that to me?"

"Is it he?"

"Is what he? What do you mean?"

"Is he your lover?"

She smiled disdainfully.

54

"A kid like him! Why, he's barely twenty!"

"At any rate, my poor child, he's the one you're trying to shield."

"I'm not trying to shield anyone. . . . And what's more, I'm not answering any more questions. . . . You've no right to harass me from morning to night, and nag and nag at me. . . . I'll lodge a complaint."

"Go ahead."

"You think you're so clever, don't you? And you're so strong. Well, any fool can bully a poor, helpless girl with no one to protect her."

He put on his hat, having made up his mind that, in spite of the rain, he was going back to the Anneau d'Or. He made for the door, without even bothering to tell her he was leaving. He had had enough. He had got it all wrong. He would have to go right back to the beginning again, and examine the facts from a fresh angle.

To hell with the rain! He took a resolute step forward, only to find Félicie clinging to his arm.

"Please don't go!"

"Why ever not?"

"You know why. . . . Don't go. . . . I'm terrified of thunder."

And it was true. For once, she was not lying. She was trembling from head to foot. Once again, she begged him to stay, and when he did reluctantly return with her to the kitchen and sit down, glowering, but sitting down all the same, she seemed genuinely grateful, and to prove it, she said:

"Would you like a cup of coffee? Can I get you a little glass of something?"

And, with a forced smile, she repeated, as she poured his coffee:

"Why are you so unkind to me? I've never done you any harm. . . ."

55

4

The Taxi

Maigret walked along Rue Pigalle at a leisurely pace, with his
hands deep in his coat pockets. It was past midnight, and,
following the storm, there was quite a chill in the air, and the
streets were still wet in places. By the light of the neon signs
the nightclub doormen were quick to recognize him, and the
customers standing at the horseshoe-shaped counter of the
tobacconist's shop on the corner of Rue Notre-Dame-de-
Lorette exchanged inquiring glances. An outsider would have
noticed nothing amiss. And yet an almost imperceptible
tremor ran through the night spots of Montmartre from end
to end, like the breeze on a pond that presages a gale.

Maigret was aware of it. It gave him considerable satisfaction. Here at least was something more manageable than a
weeping, defiant girl. He was conscious of shadowy figures
slinking past, knew that the word was being passed at lightning
speed throughout the cabarets of the district, and that here and
there lavatory attendants were hastily concealing little en-
velopes of "snow."

There to his left was the Pélican, with its blue neon sign
and its black doorman. Someone loomed up in front of him out
of the shadows, and a voice whispered:

"Am I glad to see you!"

It was Janvier. He went on to say, in those flat tones of his which to some seemed to denote callousness, but which, in fact, were merely a mannerism:

"It's in the bag, Chief. There was just one thing worrying me . . . that he would crack too soon. . . . He's at the end of his rope."

The two men stood together on the edge of the sidewalk, savoring the night air with apparent enjoyment, and Maigret refilled his pipe.

"Even before we left Rouen, I could see what a state he was in. While we were waiting for the train in the buffet, I kept expecting him to come up and buttonhole me, and get it all off his chest. . . . If ever I saw a loser, he's it. . . ."

Nothing of what was going on around him escaped Maigret. His mere presence there in the street, he knew, was having its effect. How many people with uneasy consciences were quietly making themselves scarce, or finding hiding places for things they did not want found?

"On the train, he collapsed into a heap. . . . When we got to Gare Saint-Lazare, he didn't seem to know what to do next. And besides, he was pretty drunk by then, because he'd been drinking heavily ever since yesterday. . . . Finally he went back to his place on Rue Lepic. Presumably he washed up. Anyway, he changed into his dinner jacket. . . . He picked at some food in a crummy little restaurant on Place Blanche, and then he went to work. Are you going in there? Do you want me with you?"

"Be off with you, and get some sleep, my dear fellow."

If Maigret should have need of anyone, he could always call on the two men he had kept on duty at the Quai des Orfèvres.

"Here goes!" He sighed.

As he went into the Pélican, the doorman rushed up to him, grinning from ear to ear. He shrugged. All this bogus civility was nothing new to him. He refused to surrender his coat to the coatroom attendant. Velvet curtains divided the vestibule from the cabaret. He could already hear the strains of jazz inside. A small bar on the left. Two women yawning, a drunken youth, the proprietor, bowing and scraping.

"Good evening," grunted the Chief Superintendent.

The proprietor, needless to say, was looking uneasy.

"What's up? No unpleasantness, I trust."

"No, no, of course not."

And Maigret, pushing him aside, went across and sat at a corner table not far from the band.

"Would you care for a whisky?"

"Just a small beer, thanks."

"You know very well we don't serve beer."

"A brandy-and-water, then."

It was a sorry sight that met his eyes! Such an exchange of furtive glances. Was there a single genuine customer in the whole of that cramped little room, where shaded lights cast a reddish glow that turned to violet when the band was playing a tango? There were plenty of dance hostesses. Now that they had recognized the new arrival, they were no longer bothering to dance together. One of them even went so far as to get out her crochetwork.

On stage, Pétillon, in his dinner jacket, looked even younger and thinner than he really was. His face was as white as a sheet beneath his long fair hair, and his eyelids were red from fatigue and anxiety. Try as he would, he could not keep his eyes off the Chief Superintendent, waiting patiently in his corner.

Janvier was right; it was in the bag. The signs were unmistakable. Here was a man who had reached the end of his rope. He was falling apart. His head was swimming. There was only one thing he wanted now: to unburden himself of the load on his conscience, and the sooner the better. So much so that at one point it really looked as if Jacques Pétillon was about to lay down his saxophone and hasten to Maigret's side.

It was not a pretty sight, a man convulsed with terror. He was not the first whom Maigret had seen in this state. At times, he himself had cunningly manipulated an interrogation—which might last for twenty hours or more—to induce in his suspect, or, one could almost say, his patient, just such a condition of physical and moral collapse.

In this case he was in no way responsible. As a suspect, Pétillon had not interested him. Instinctively, he had felt that he was of no account. He had ignored him, mesmerized instead by that enigmatic girl, Félicie, whom he could still not get out of his mind.

He sipped his drink. His air of unconcern must have astonished Pétillon. His hands, with their long thin fingers, were shaking, and the other members of the band were watching him, and exchanging sidelong glances.

What had he been searching for in the past tumultuous forty-eight hours? What desperate hope had he clung to? What face had he expected to see as he watched the comings and goings in a bar or a café, his feverish gaze riveted on the door? Time and time again, he had been disappointed and gone elsewhere to resume his search, finally ending up in Rouen, in a brasserie near the Barracks frequented by prostitutes.

He was squeezed dry. If Maigret had not come for him, he would have given himself up, stumbling up the dusty staircase of Police Headquarters, and demanding to be given a hearing.

This was it! The band was taking a few minutes off. The accordion player went across to the bar for a drink. The others chatted in undertones. Pétillon laid down his instrument and came down the two steps leading from the stage.

"I must talk to you!" he stammered.

The Chief Superintendent replied, sounding very kind and gentle:

"I know, young fellow."

Here? Maigret looked around at the revolting décor. The last thing he wanted was for the poor boy to make a spectacle of himself in public, especially since he was so obviously close to tears.

"Thirsty?"

Pétillon shook his head.

"In that case, let's get out of here."

Maigret paid for his drink, in spite of the proprietor's protests that it was on the house.

"Look, I think the band will have to do without you for the rest of the night. You and I are going to take a little walk, just the two of us. . . . Get your hat and coat, Pétillon."

"I haven't got a coat."

As soon as they were outside, he took a deep breath, as if about to execute a high dive, and began:

"Listen, Chief Superintendent . . . I'll tell you the whole story. . . . I've had about as much as I can take. . . ."

He was trembling from head to foot. The streetlights were no doubt swimming before his eyes. The proprietor of the Pélican and the doorman watched as they walked away.

"Take your time, son."

He was taking him to the Quai des Orfèvres. It would make it easier for both of them. Maigret could not count the number of times he had known a case to end like this, late at night, in his own office, after everyone had gone home except for one man on duty at the desk in the hall. He could not remember how often he had seen the eerie light of his green-shaded lamp reflected on the face of a broken man.

This one was just a boy. Maigret felt disgruntled, reflecting that the characters in this particular drama were a decidedly feeble lot.

60

"We're going in here. . . ."

He nudged him toward a brasserie on Place Pigalle, feeling badly in need of a glass of beer before hailing a taxi to take them to the Quai des Orfèvres.

"What will you have?"

"Anything. It doesn't matter. . . . I swear to you, Chief Superintendent, that I didn't . . ."

"I know. . . . I know. . . . You'll tell me all about it later. . . . Waiter! Two beers."

Maigret shrugged. Two more people had recognized him, and had abandoned their *soupe à l'oignon* to get away from him.

The hunched back of one of them could be seen in the telephone booth as he called for a taxi.

"Is she your mistress?"

"Who?"

Well, well! The boy really had no idea what he was talking about. There was no mistaking the genuineness of his bewilderment.

"Félicie."

And Pétillon, as if confronted for the first time with a notion that had never even crossed his mind, repeated:

"Félicie, my mistress?"

He was utterly at sea. He had been on the very brink of a sensational confession, and here was this fellow Maigret, who had set half the police force of Paris on his track, and who held his fate in his hands, babbling about his uncle's servant girl!

"I swear to you, Chief Superintendent . . ."

"Good . . . Let's be going, anyway. . . ."

Ears were flapping. Two women nearby, while pretending to repair their make-up, were listening for all they were worth. They would be better off without an audience.

They were out in the street once more. A few yards away,

in darkened Place Pigalle, was a taxi stand. Maigret started to raise his arm to summon one. Close by, a policeman on foot patrol gazed absently into space.

And at that precise second, a shot rang out. The Chief Superintendent was conscious, at almost the same moment, of another sound, that of a taxi driving off toward Boulevard Rochechouart.

It all happened so quickly that he did not immediately register the fact that his companion's hand had flown to his chest, and that he was swaying on his feet, groping with his other hand for something to hold on to. Mechanically, he asked:

"Are you hit?"

The policeman hurried off toward the taxi stand. He opened the door of the first cab, sprang into the driver's seat, and drove off fast. The taxi driver, taking it in the right spirit, leaped onto the running board.

Pétillon, his hand pressed to his starched shirt front, fell to the ground. He attempted to cry out, but the only sound he managed to produce was an odd, pitifully faint little gurgle.

Next morning, the newspapers reported the incident baldly in a paragraph inconspicuously tucked away:

Last night, in Place Pigalle, Jacques P., a jazz musician, was shot in the chest by an unknown assailant, who escaped in a taxi. A policeman on duty at the time immediately gave chase, but was unable to catch up with the gunman.

It is presumed that the motive was either revenge or jealousy.

The wounded man, whose condition is said to be serious, was taken to Beaujon Hospital. The police are continuing their inquiries.

It was not wholly accurate. Police handouts to the press seldom are. It was true that Jacques Pétillon was in Beaujon

Hospital. It was true that his condition was serious, so serious that it might not be possible to save his life. His left lung had been perforated by a large bullet.

As to the story of the police giving chase, that was a different matter. At the daily briefing that morning, Maigret had sounded bitter when he discussed the matter with the Chief Commissioner.

"I blame myself, Chief. . . . I was dying for a beer, and I persuaded myself that it would give the boy a chance to pull himself together before I brought him here. . . . He was on the verge of collapse. He hadn't had a minute's respite all day. . . . I was wrong, of course. . . .

"The man must have seen his chance, and wasted no time. He wasn't born yesterday, you can be sure of that.

"When I heard the shot, I had no thought but for the boy. . . . I left it to the foot policeman to give chase. . . . Have you read his report? The taxi led him on a wild-goose chase to Place d'Italie, right at the other side of Paris. Then it came to an abrupt stop, and it turned out that there was no one in it but the driver.

"The driver, protesting his innocence, was brought in for questioning. . . . Oh, well, however you look at it, I was well and truly led by the nose. . . ."

Irately, he glanced through the taxi driver's statement.

"I was in my cab at the stand in Place Pigalle when I was approached by a man I didn't know, who offered me two hundred francs to help him play a joke on a friend. That's what he said, anyway. He was to set off a firecracker—his exact words again—and the bang was to be the signal for me to drive at full speed as far as Place d'Italie. . . ."

A little too forthcoming for a taxi driver on the night shift! Still, it would be difficult to prove that he was lying.

"I couldn't see the man very clearly. I was parked in the shadow of the trees, and besides, he was careful to keep his head down. He was broad-shouldered and was wearing a dark suit and a gray hat."

A description that would fit almost anyone!

"I won't forget that setup in a hurry, I can promise you," grumbled Maigret. "I can't deny that it was ingenious. The fellow had only to keep out of sight, crouched between two taxis, or in any patch of shade. . . . He shoots. . . . And instantly, the taxi moves off, and, as is to be expected, everyone assumes that the murderer is inside. The policeman on the spot sets off in pursuit, leaving our villain at leisure to slink away or melt into the crowd, as he chooses. . . . The other drivers at the stand have been questioned. None of them saw anything. . . . Except one old fellow—I've known him for years—who thinks he spotted a shadowy figure lurking near the fountain."

And to think that the saxophone player had been ready to talk, willing to tell the whole story, right there in the Pélican, and it had been Maigret himself who had shut him up! Now, God alone could tell when, if ever, it would be possible to take a statement from him.

"What are you proposing to do?"

There was a standard procedure in such cases. The incident had occurred in Montmartre, within a narrowly circumscribed area. The next step was to pull in for questioning some fifty men, all of them known to the police, who had been seen in the locality on the night in question, and who had scurried hither and thither like scalded cats the moment word had got around that Chief Superintendent Maigret was in the vicinity of Place Pigalle.

Some of these men were hardened criminals. Lean on them a little, threaten them with closer investigation into their affairs, and they would be only too willing to tell what they knew.

"I'll put a couple of men on it, Chief. As for myself . . ."

He could not help himself; his thoughts were elsewhere.

Right from the start! Ever since he had first set foot in that cardboard cutout of a place called Jeanneville.

Surely his reluctance to leave the vicinity of Cape Horn and Félicie, with all her inconsistencies, had amounted almost to a presentiment?

Events had proved him wrong. It now seemed almost certain that it was in the area of Place Pigalle that the solution to the mystery of old Lapie's death was to be found.

"All the same, I'm going back there."

Pétillon had had time to tell him just one thing: Félicie was not his mistress. He had been flabbergasted at the very suggestion, as if such a thought had never so much as entered his mind.

It was half past eight. Maigret telephoned his wife.

"Is that you? . . . No, nothing special . . . I don't know when I'll be back."

His erratic comings and goings were nothing new to her. He fished a bundle of reports out of his pocket. Among them was one from Rouen, which included the life history of all the women who plied their trade at the Tivoli. Pétillon had not "gone upstairs" with any of them. He had gone into the brasserie and sat down on one of the corner benches upholstered in crimson velvet. Presently, two of the women had gone over to him and sat down on either side of him.

"I'm looking for a girl by the name of Adèle," he had said.

"You've left it a bit late, love. Adèle hasn't worked here for ages. You do mean the little dark one with pear-shaped tits, don't you?"

He didn't know. All he knew was that he was looking for a girl named Adèle who had worked there about a year ago. But she had left some months before, and no one knew where she had gone. It would be a hopeless undertaking to try to track down every Adèle in every brothel in France.

An inspector would be detailed to make a thorough search

of the saxophone player's room in Rue Lepic. Janvier, who would not be able to get as much rest as he would have liked, would spend the day combing the Place Pigalle area.

As for Maigret, he took the train once more from Gare Saint-Lazare, got off at Poissy, and toiled up the hill to Jeanneville.

After last night's storm, the grass looked even greener, and the sky a softer blue. Soon the colored houses came into view, and, as he went past her shop, he waved to Mélanie Chochoi, who was looking vacantly out the window.

He was going to see Félicie. He was looking forward to it with pleasure. Why, he wondered. Involuntarily, his pace quickened. He smiled as he thought of Lucas, who was no doubt fed up again after a night spent on guard outside Cape Horn. He could see him in the distance, sitting on the grass verge, with an unlit pipe in his mouth. He must be longing for some sleep and something to eat.

"Well, how are things, my poor Lucas?"

"Dead quiet, Chief. I could do with a cup of coffee and a few hours in bed. . . . But first, coffee."

His eyes were puffy from lack of sleep, his coat crumpled, and his shoes and the bottoms of his trousers spattered with reddish mud.

"It's back to the Anneau d'Or for you. . . . There's been a new development."

"What's happened?"

"The saxophone player has been shot in the chest."

The Chief Superintendent sounded indifferent, but Sergeant Lucas was not deceived, and he went off shaking his head.

Well, here he was! Maigret looked around him with the satisfaction engendered by familiar surroundings, and went toward the front door of the cottage. But, on second thought, no. He decided he would prefer to go around to the back and in through the garden. He opened the gate. The kitchen door stood open.

Then he stood stock still and gaped stupidly, feeling well-nigh uncontrollable laughter rising in his throat. At the sound of his footsteps, Félicie had come to the door, and she stood there in the doorway, her back very straight, looking at him with a severe expression on her face.

But, good God, what was wrong with her? What had she done to her face? Her eyes were swollen and her cheeks streaked with red, but, this time, not from weeping.

As he came nearer, she said, sounding even more acid than usual:

"Well, I hope you're satisfied now."

"What happened? Did you fall downstairs?"

"A fat lot of good it did, leaving a policeman on guard night and day outside the house! Some watchdog! He was asleep at the time, I daresay!"

"See here, Félicie, you'd better stop talking in riddles. You're not trying to tell me . . ."

"That the murderer came here and attacked me? Yes! Isn't that what you wanted?"

Maigret had meant to tell her about the attempted murder of Pétillon, but he decided to postpone it until he had learned more about what had been happening at Cape Horn.

"Come and sit down. . . . Out here in the garden, yes . . . Don't look like that! Stop glowering at me, do, and just tell me, as calmly as you can, exactly what happened. Last night, when I left here, you were in a highly nervous state. What did you do?"

Contemptuously, she replied:

"Nothing."

"Very well. You had your dinner, I presume. Then you locked up the house and went up to bed. That's right, isn't it? Are you sure you locked all the doors?"

"I always lock the doors before I go to bed."

"So you went to bed. What time was that?"

"I stayed downstairs until the storm was over."

It was true that he had been heartless enough to walk out on her, knowing full well how terrified she was of thunder and lightning.

"Did you have anything to drink?"

"Just some coffee."

"To help you sleep, no doubt! And then?"

"I read."

"For how long?"

"I don't know. Maybe till about midnight. I put the light out. I was sure something dreadful was going to happen. I warned you!"

"Well, now you can tell me all about it."

"You're making fun of me. . . . But I don't care. . . . You think you're so clever, don't you? . . . Sometime later, I heard a sort of scratching sound in Monsieur Lapie's bedroom. . . ."

Maigret did not believe a word of her story, and as he listened, watching her face all the while, he was wondering what she hoped to gain by this new pack of lies. For lying came as naturally to her as breathing. In response to his inquiries, the Superintendent of Police in Fécamp had supplied him over the telephone with certain facts.

Maigret now knew that Félicie's sly hints about her relationship with Jules Lapie were pure invention. She had a perfectly good father and mother of her own. Her mother was a washerwoman, and her father a drunken good-for-nothing, who loafed about the waterfront, doing odd jobs here and there, especially if there was any free drink being handed out. Questioning the neighbors had yielded no results. Even the most blatant gossips could suggest no link between old Lapie and the washerwoman. It was simply that, hearing that his brother was looking for a girl to keep house for him, the ship's carpenter had recommended Félicie, who was employed by him to help part time with the housework.

"You were saying, my child, that you heard a scratching sound. So, naturally, you went straight to the window and called for help to the policeman outside. . . ."

Her only response to this heavy sarcasm was a shake of her head.

"Why ever not?"

"Because."

"Because, I presume, you thought you knew who was in the room next door, and you didn't want him arrested?"

"Maybe."

"Go on."

"I crept out of bed without making a sound."

"And without turning on the light, I don't doubt. Because if you had, Sergeant Lucas would have spotted it. The shutters don't quite meet in the middle. . . . Anyway, you got out of bed. . . . Weren't you frightened? Or is it only thunder and lightning you're afraid of? . . . What happened next? Did you come out of your room?"

"Not right away. I put my ear to the door and listened. I could hear someone moving about across the landing. . . . I heard a chair scrape, and then what sounded like a muffled oath. . . . I realized that the man, whoever it was, had not found what he was looking for, and that he was getting ready to leave."

"Had you locked your bedroom door?"

"Yes."

"And then you opened it and, without any sort of weapon to protect yourself, you flew out to confront the intruder, who might well be the man who had murdered Jules Lapie?"

"Yes."

She spoke defiantly. He gave an admiring little whistle. "I take it, then, that you were quite confident that he

69

wouldn't harm you? Needless to say, you couldn't possibly have guessed that, at the material time, young Pétillon was miles away in Paris."

Involuntarily she exclaimed:

"What do you know about it?"

"Let's see . . . what time would this have been?"

"I didn't look at the time until *afterward*. By then, it was half past three in the morning. . . . How do you know that Jacques . . . ?"

"Oh, so you're on first-name terms, are you?"

"Oh, for heaven's sake, stop it! If you don't believe me, go away and leave me alone."

"Sorry. I won't interrupt you again. . . . You were very brave. You came out of your room armed only with your courage, and . . ."

"He smashed his fist into my face!"

"And then took to his heels?"

"He ran out through the garden gate. . . . That's how he got in."

Maigret was sorely tempted to say, in spite of the bruises on her face:

"Well, my dear, you might as well know that I don't believe a word of it."

If he had been told that she had inflicted the injuries on herself, he would have been quite prepared to believe it. Why?

But, no sooner had the thought crossed his mind than his eye was caught by something in a flower bed. Following his glance, she saw what he had seen, footprints in the still-damp earth.

Her lips twitched in a little smile, as she said:

"My footprints, would you say?"

He stood up.

"Come with me."

He went into the house. More muddy footprints were

70

clearly to be seen on the highly polished treads of the staircase. He went into the old man's bedroom.

"Did you come in here at all?"

"Yes, but I didn't touch anything."

"This chair here—was it in this same position last night?"

"No. It was over by the window."

It was now pushed up against the huge walnut wardrobe, and besides, mudstains were clearly visible on the rush matting on the floor.

So Félicie had been telling the truth, after all. A man really had broken into Cape Horn in the night, and that man could not possibly have been Pétillon, since he, poor fellow, at the time had been lying on an operating table in Beaujon Hospital.

If Maigret needed further proof, he found it when he got up on the chair and examined the top of the wardrobe, where the thick coating of dust was crisscrossed with finger marks. Maigret noted also that one of the boards had been loosened with a tool of some sort.

He would have to get the Forensic Laboratory people on to it, to take photographs and test for fingerprints, if any.

Looking pensive and wearing a troubled frown, Maigret murmured, as if to himself:

"And you didn't call for help! You knew that there was a policeman right under your window, and you didn't utter a sound. You even took care not to turn on any lights."

"I did in the kitchen, when I went down there to bathe my face in cold water."

"Ah! But then, the kitchen light couldn't be seen from the street, could it? In other words, you deliberately failed to give the alarm. In spite of the fact that he attacked you, you were determined to give your assailant enough time to get away. This morning you got up as usual, as if nothing had happened, and still you said not a word to the Sergeant."

71

"I knew very well that you would come back!"

In an odd sort of way—he knew that it was childish of him, and was a little ashamed of himself—he felt flattered that she should have waited for him to arrive, rather than turn to Lucas for help. He was even secretly touched by her words:

"I knew very well that you would come back!"

He went out of the room, locking the door behind him. At all events, the mysterious intruder had not extended his search from the top of the wardrobe. No drawers had been opened. Nothing had been disarranged. Which must mean that he knew . . .

When they returned to the kitchen, Félicie glanced at her bruised face in the mirror.

"You told me just now that you were with Jacques last night."

He looked at her searchingly. She was really upset, no doubt about it. She waited in anguish for him to speak. When at last he did, he said, making it sound as casual as he could:

"You assured me yesterday that he was not your lover, that to you he was just a kid. . . ."

She did not reply.

"Last night there was an accident. . . . Some unknown person shot at him in the street."

She gave a cry.

"Is he dead? Tell me! Is Jacques dead?"

He was sorely tempted. When had she ever scrupled to lie to him? In police work, surely everything was permissible in the interests of bringing the criminal to justice? It was on the tip of his tongue to say "yes." How would she react? Who could tell but that . . . ?

But he hadn't the heart to go through with it. She was upset enough already. Turning his head away, he mumbled:

"No, don't distress yourself. . . . He's not dead. Only wounded . . ."

She began sobbing. With her hands to her forehead and her eyes wild, she wailed distractedly:

"Jacques! Jacques! Oh, my darling Jacques!"

In a sudden burst of fury, she turned on this imperturbable man, who persisted in avoiding her eyes:

"And you were there with him, weren't you? And you let it happen! I hate you, do you hear? I hate you. It's all because of you, yes, because of you. . . ."

She collapsed into a chair, and went on sobbing, slumped over the kitchen table with her head against the coffee grinder.

Every now and then, she repeated:

"Jacques! My darling Jacques!"

Was Maigret really as hard-hearted as she supposed? Be that as it may, he stood for a while in the doorway, hardly knowing where to look, then went out into the deserted garden, prowled around for a minute or two, hesitated, peered at his shadow on the ground, and finally went into the cellar and poured himself a glass of wine.

This was not the first time he had seen Félicie cry. But her tears today were of a different kind.

5

Number 13

Maigret's patience, that morning, was inexhaustible. All the same! He had not been able to prevent Félicie from wearing her full mourning outfit, including the absurd flat black hat with the crepe veil, which floated like the draperies on a Grecian frieze. And what on earth had she done to her face? Had she merely tried to cover up her bruises? It was impossible to tell with her, her sense of the dramatic being so highly developed. Whatever the reason, her face was dead white, as thickly daubed with grease and powder as the face of a clown. In the train on the way to Paris she sat motionless, like a priestess, her melancholy gaze fixed on distant horizons, the whole effect deliberately contrived to evoke the response:

"Good God! How she must be suffering! . . . And what admirable self-control! She is the very embodiment of anguish. Our Lady of Sorrows in the flesh!"

And yet, not once did Maigret permit himself so much as the ghost of a smile. When they came to a grocer's in Rue du Faubourg-Saint-Honoré, and she wanted to go in, he murmured kindly:

"I don't think he's in a fit condition to eat anything, my dear."

Was he being obtuse, then? No, he understood and, seeing that she persisted, let her have her way. She bought a bunch of the finest Spanish grapes, some oranges, and a bottle of champagne. She insisted on buying flowers as well, a huge bunch of white lilac, and she staggered along, carrying it all herself, and still looking like the Tragic Muse incarnate.

Maigret trotted along at her heels, resigned and indulgent, like any fond papa. He was relieved to find, when they arrived at Beaujon Hospital, that visitors were not admitted at this hour, for, looking the way she did, Félicie would have given the patients a shock. He was, however, able to persuade the house surgeon to arrange for her to catch a glimpse of Jacques Pétillon in his cubicle, which was right at the end of a long corridor, gleaming with glossy paint and filled with stale smells, with open doors at either side, through which could be seen rows of beds, wan faces, and white walls, white linen, and white equipment, too much white altogether, for white, in this place, was the color of pain.

They were kept waiting for some considerable time, and all the while she just stood there, clutching her parcels. At long last, a nurse appeared. She looked at Félicie, gave a little start, and exclaimed:

"I'll take all that stuff. . . . It will do for the children's ward. . . . Shh! You mustn't talk. Don't make a sound."

She opened the door the merest crack, so that Félicie could see little in the darkened cubicle but the dim figure of Pétillon, motionless as a corpse.

Then the nurse shut the door again, whereupon Félicie saw fit to say:

"You will save him, won't you? I beg you, I implore you, do everything you can to save his life."

"But, mademoiselle . . ."

"Spare no expense. . . . Here . . ."

Maigret did not laugh, he did not even smile, when she

took a thousand-franc note, folded over many times, and held it out to the nurse.

"If it's a question of money, whatever the amount . . ."

Even though she had never appeared more extravagantly ridiculous, she was no longer a figure of fun to Maigret. More than that, he felt positively protective toward her. As they went back down the corridor, with Félicie's black veil floating luxuriantly behind her, a child stepped into her path. She bent down to kiss the little patient, and sighed.

"Poor little mite!"

Surely the suffering of others is especially painful to those who have themselves suffered? Close by stood a young nurse with platinum-blonde hair, wearing an outrageously tight and revealing coverall. She watched the scene with a barely stifled giggle, and called out to a colleague in one of the wards to come and see the fun.

"You ought to be ashamed of yourself, young woman!" admonished Maigret. And he stalked off with Félicie like a hen with one chick. Félicie had heard the reprimand, and she was grateful to him. Outside in the sunlit street, she was visibly more relaxed. She seemed to feel that there was a kind of bond between them, and he took advantage of this to murmur:

"You know the whole truth, don't you?"

She did not deny it. Shamefacedly, she averted her eyes.

"Come on."

It was a little short of midday. Maigret decided to take a turning to the right and join the noisy and colorful throng in Place des Ternes. She followed him, teetering on her excessively high heels.

"But you won't get anything out of me," she said a few moments later.

"I know."

By now, he knew a great many things. He did not yet know the name of old Lapie's murderer, or of the man who had shot the saxophone player the previous night, but that was only a matter of time.

What he did know was that Félicie . . . How could he express it? On the train, for instance, the other people in the car, observing her theatrical pose of frozen grief, had thought her absurd; in the hospital, the pert little nurse had giggled helplessly; the proprietor of the dance hall in Poissy had nicknamed her the Parakeet; others called her the Princess; and Lapie had called her his Poll Parrot. Maigret himself had been thoroughly irritated by her childish posturing.

Even now, people were turning around to look at them, and they certainly did make an odd couple. And when Maigret ushered her into a little restaurant, mostly patronized by regulars, but empty at this time of day, he caught the waiter winking at the proprietor, seated behind the cash desk.

What Maigret had discovered was quite simply that under even the most preposterous exterior, there beats a human heart.

"What do you say to having a nice, quiet lunch with me?"

Mechanically, she repeated:

"I won't tell you anything, just the same."

"I understand, child. You won't tell me anything. What will you have to eat?"

The little restaurant was cozy and rather shabby, with yellowing white walls, and a number of large, somewhat tarnished mirrors. Here and there stood globular nickel-plated receptacles, in which the waiter disposed of the dirty table linen. Behind the cash desk were pigeonholes, painted to look like wood, in which the regular customers' table napkins were kept. The plat du jour, which was *Navarin printanier,* was chalked up on the wall. On the menu, supplementary prices had been written in next to almost all the dishes.

Maigret gave the order. Félicie flung back her veil, and its weight pulled back the hair on her forehead.

"Were you very miserable in Fécamp?"

He knew what he was doing. He was quite prepared for the tremor of her lips, and the defiant expression on her face, which was almost second nature to her.

"Why should I have been?"

Of course! Why should she? He knew Fécamp well, with its mean, cramped little terraced houses huddled at the foot of the cliffs, upstream from the estuary, its streets awash with dirty water, and its children playing amid the sickening stench of fish.

"How many brothers and sisters have you?"

"Seven."

The drink-sodden father. The mother at her washtub from morning till night. He could imagine her, an overgrown, skinny child with thin legs and bare feet. She had been put to work as a menial in a little waterfront restaurant, Chez Arsène, where she was housed in the attic. She had been dismissed because she had pinched a few sous from the till. Subsequently, she had been employed as a daily help by Ernest Lapie, the ship's carpenter.

She was eating now, very daintily, though not actually with her little finger stuck out. Maigret felt no inclination to laugh.

"I could have married the son of a shipowner, if I'd wanted to."

"I'm sure you could, child. But you refused him, is that it?"

"I don't like redheads. And besides, his father made a pass at me. Men are such pigs. . . ."

It was an odd thing, but from some angles she looked so much younger than her twenty-four years, more like a high-strung twelve-year-old, and it was difficult to imagine how anyone could take her seriously.

"Tell me, Félicie. Was your employer—sorry, Peg Leg, I

78

should say—was Peg Leg of a jealous disposition?"

He felt very pleased with himself. She was reacting as he had expected, chin up, eyes blazing with anger, a look of mingled surprise and anxiety.

"There was never anything between us."

"I know, child. But that didn't prevent him from being jealous, did it? I bet you anything you like that he forbade you to go dancing in Poissy on your Sundays off, and that you had to slip away without telling him."

She did not reply. Doubtless, she was wondering how he could possibly have found out about the old man's perverse jealousy, which drove him to spy on her, to go to meet her on her way back on Sunday nights, and to make the most frightful scenes.

"You led him to believe that you had more than one lover. . . ."

"Why shouldn't I have lovers?"

"Why not, indeed! And you told him all about them. And he called you every name under the sun. I wonder he didn't take a strap to you."

"He wouldn't have dared touch me. . . ."

She was lying. Maigret could just see the two of them. They were as cut off from the rest of the world, in the newly built cottage in the middle of the Jeanneville Estate, as if they had been shipwrecked together on a desert island. Neither had any ties elsewhere. From morning to night, they spied on each other, and quarreled and fought, because they needed each other. In fact, they were everything to one another.

The only escape for Peg Leg was his nightly game of cards at the Anneau d'Or, but Félicie's bids for freedom were altogether noisier and more spectacular.

The old man was forced to lock her in her room and stand guard under her window to prevent her from slipping away to the dance hall in Poissy on Sundays, to play the part of a princess in disguise. Every other free moment she could get was spent in pouring out the secrets of her heart to her bosom friend, Léontine.

It was all so simple, really. One after another, the humble, hard-working regular patrons of the restaurant came in to have their lunch and read their newspapers. But there was not one who did not gape in bewilderment at the extravagant creature who looked so out of place in these familiar surroundings, not one who, glancing covertly at Félicie from time to time, was not tempted to smile and exchange a wink with the waiter.

And yet she was just a woman, or, rather, a child on the brink of womanhood. This was what Maigret had seen in her, which was why his manner toward her was now so gentle, so indulgent, so affectionate.

Around her, he was beginning to reconstruct the daily life of Cape Horn. Had old Lapie still been alive, Maigret would certainly not have scrupled to scandalize the old man by accusing him outright:

"You're eaten up with jealousy where that girl is concerned!"

Jealous! How could he be jealous, when he had never even been in love in his whole life? But jealous he was, nonetheless, because she was a part of his world, such a narrow little world that to deprive him of so much as a fragment of it would mean a fearful loss to him.

When had he ever sold his surplus vegetables, or the fruit from his orchard? Or even given them away? Never! They were his property. Félicie, too, was his property. Strangers were not made welcome in his house. He and he alone had drunk the wine in his cellar.

"How did he come to invite his nephew to stay?"

"He went to see him in Paris. . . . He had wanted him to come to Cape Horn after his sister died. But Jacques wouldn't hear of it. . . . He had his pride. . . ."

"And one day, when Lapie was on one of his quarterly visits to Paris to collect his compensation, he went to see his nephew, and found him in a pitiful state, isn't that so?"

"What do you mean by that?"

"Pétillon had been reduced to unloading vegetables in Les Halles."

"There's nothing to be ashamed of in that!"

"Of course not. Nothing whatever. Quite the reverse. Anyway, he brought him home. He gave up his own room to him, because . . ."

She was outraged.

"It wasn't like that at all!"

"All the same, he did keep a very close eye on you both. . . . What did he find out?"

"Nothing."

"Were you Pétillon's mistress?"

She looked down at her plate, neither confirming nor denying it.

"Be that as it may, the fact is that life became impossible for Pétillon, and he left the house."

"He and his uncle didn't see eye to eye. . . ."

"That's what I'm saying."

Maigret felt a glow of contentment. He would always remember this simple meal in the restful, commonplace surroundings of the little restaurant, mainly patronized by regulars. A slanting sunbeam flickered on the tablecloth and on the carafe of red wine. A pleasant, almost cordial intimacy had developed between himself and Félicie. He knew well enough that if he ventured to refer to it, she would resume her disdainful manner, and deny it vehemently. Yet she was enjoying herself as much as he was, thankful for a respite from her solitary life, and the chaotic fantasies with which she filled it.

"It will all sort itself out in the end. You'll see."

She was almost ready to believe him. But her mistrustful nature was too strong for her. She was still afraid of stumbling into some sort of trap. Every now and then—but alas, not for long—she seemed on the point of letting go, and behaving normally, like any other girl. She was within a hair's breadth of relaxing completely, of looking at Maigret without affectation, and saying what she really felt. Tears welled up in her eyes; a softer, more resigned expression spread over her features.

She was about to confide in him, and he was only too willing to help her, to be a father to her. . . .

But at the very last minute, her wariness got the upper hand again. She looked more stubborn than ever, and she said, in her most acid tones:

"You needn't think I don't know what you're up to."

She felt so alone. Only she was burdened with the whole weight of the tragedy. She was right at the very center of things. Surely the fact that a chief superintendent of the Police Judiciaire, a celebrity like Maigret, spent all his time harassing her and her alone was proof enough of that!

Little did she suspect that her companion, even now, was pulling a great many other strings. He had inspectors digging away in Place Pigalle and thereabouts. At the Quai des Orfèvres, a number of dubious characters, hustled out of bed in their sleazy lodgings in the small hours, were being interrogated. In various provincial towns, officers of the Vice Squad were searching for a girl named Adèle, who had recently spent several months working in a brasserie in Rouen.

All this was standard police procedure, and was bound, in the end, to yield results.

But sitting here in this little restaurant, where the regulars greeted one another with no more than a discreet nod—for, although they had seen each other every single day at lunchtime for years, they had not been introduced—the Chief Superintendent was not concerned with the mechanics of detection, but with the essential nature of the crime.

"Do you like strawberries?"

There were several punnets of them on the sideboard, packed in cotton wool, the first of the season.

"Waiter . . . bring us some strawberries."

It amused him to see how she relished them. It was not so much that she was greedy as that expensive delicacies appealed to her imagination. It was of little consequence that Jacques Pétillon was in no condition to enjoy grapes, oranges, or champagne. It was the gesture that was important, and the sight of the big purple fruit and the gold cap on the bottle. She might or might not like strawberries, but she was certainly eating them with enjoyment.

"What's wrong, child?"

"Nothing."

She had suddenly turned very pale, and this time it was not an act. She had had a shock. She choked on a mouthful of fruit, and seemed on the point of scrambling to her feet and bolting. She coughed and hid her face in her handkerchief, pretending that all that was amiss was that something had gone down the wrong way.

"What on earth . . . ?"

Turning around, Maigret saw a small man wearing, in spite of the mildness of the weather, a heavy overcoat and a muffler. The man took them off, hung them on a coat peg, and collected a rolled table napkin from the pigeonhole numbered thirteen.

He was middle-aged, graying, ordinary, one of those colorless people so often to be found in large towns, lonely, fussy, touchy characters, widowers or hardened bachelors, whose lives consisted of a succession of familiar little rituals. The waiter served him without showing him a menu, and brought him an open bottle of mineral water. The man, just as he was about to open his newspaper, caught sight of Félicie, and frowned, as if trying to remember, asking himself . . .

"Aren't you going to finish your strawberries?"

"I've had enough. Let's go."

She had already put her napkin down on the table. Her hand was trembling.

"Calm down, my dear."

"Me? I'm perfectly calm. Why ever shouldn't I be?"

From where he was sitting, Maigret was able to see the man's reflection in the mirror opposite. His face was still working as he tried to place the vaguely familiar features. Was it . . . ? No . . . Had she . . . ? No, that wasn't it. . . . Come on! He went on trying to figure it out. He was almost there. . . . There! He had it! His eyes widened. It had quite shaken him. He seemed to be saying to himself:

"Good heavens! What an extraordinary coincidence!"

But he did not move from his seat. He did not nod or smile, or show any outward sign of recognition. Where had they met? And in what circumstances? The man was staring searchingly at Maigret. He summoned the waiter, and whispered something to him. The waiter must have said that he didn't know, that he had never seen either of them before.

And while all this was going on, Félicie, sick with apprehension, had suddenly got to her feet and stumbled off to the ladies' room. Had she received such a shock that she was going to bring up the strawberries, which, so short a time ago, she had been savoring with such refined enjoyment?

During her absence, Maigret and the unknown man looked at one another with undisguised curiosity. Number 13 looked as if he were sorely tempted to go across and speak to Félicie's companion.

The frosted-glass door leading to the rest rooms also led to the kitchens. The waiter came and went constantly. He had red hair. Like the shipowner's son in Fécamp who had wanted to marry Félicie. Maigret could not help smiling. Everything she saw was fuel for her imagination. She had seen a redheaded waiter. Then Maigret had asked her if she had been very miserable in Fécamp. At lightning speed, her imagination had transformed the waiter into the shipowner's son who . . .

She had been away a long time, and Maigret was beginning to feel uneasy. The waiter, too, had been absent longer than usual. Number 13 was looking very thoughtful, like a man on the brink of a momentous decision.

At long last, she reappeared. She was almost smiling. As she came toward him, she pulled her veil down over her face. She did not sit down.

"Shall we go?"

"I've ordered coffee. You like coffee, don't you?"

"Not now. It's bad for my nerves."

Pretending to be taken in, he summoned the waiter, and, as he was paying the bill, subjected him to a searching glance. The waiter flushed a little. It was all so obvious. Clearly, she had entrusted him with a message for Number 13. Probably she had scribbled a note on a scrap of paper and told him not to hand it to the man until after they had left the restaurant.

On the way out, the Chief Superintendent glanced absently at the thick overcoat, with its bulging pockets, hanging on the coat peg.

"We can go back to Jeanneville now, can't we?"

She took his arm in what might have been a spontaneous manner.

"I'm so tired. . . . It's all been so distressing."

Seeing him standing irresolutely on the edge of the sidewalk, as if undecided as to what to do next, she could scarcely conceal her impatience.

"Why are you just standing there? What're you thinking? The next train leaves in half an hour."

She was absolutely terrified. Her hand shook on Maigret's

arm. Suddenly, strangely, all that mattered to Maigret was to reassure her. He shrugged.

"What the hell! Taxi! Gare Saint-Lazare, Suburban Line."

He could only guess at the enormity of the weight that he had lifted from her shoulders. There in the open taxi, with the sunlight streaming in, words poured out:

"You promised you wouldn't leave me. . . . That's what you said, wasn't it? You're not afraid of being compromised, are you? Are you married? How stupid of me; of course you are, otherwise you wouldn't be wearing a wedding ring."

A little tremor of fear at the station. He had bought only one ticket. Did he mean to bundle her into the train, and stay behind in Paris himself? She had forgotten that he carried an official travel pass. He slumped down beside her on the seat and looked at her with a faint stirring of remorse.

As to the elderly gentleman whom he thought of as Number 13, he could lay hands on him whenever he chose, seeing that he was one of the regulars at the little restaurant. The train moved off, and Félicie believed herself out of danger. In Poissy, as they walked past the dance hall together, the proprietor, standing outside the rickety wooden building, recognized Maigret, and winked at him.

The Chief Superintendent succumbed to an irresistible urge to tease Félicie a little.

"D'you know, I think I'd like a word with him. I want to ask him whether he ever caught Peg Leg spying on you while you were dancing."

She tugged impatiently at his arm.

"You can save yourself the trouble. He followed me here several times."

"You see! I said he was of a jealous disposition, didn't I?"

They walked up the hill. As they went past Mélanie

Chochoi's shop, Maigret had another little dig at her:

"What if I were to go in and ask her how often she had seen you and Jacques Pétillon roaming about together at night?"

"She never saw us!"

This time, she spoke with absolute conviction.

"You took good care she shouldn't, is that what you mean?"

They were now in sight of the house. One of the big trucks from the Forensic Laboratory was just driving away, and Lucas was standing alone at the front door, looking as if he owned the place.

"What was that truck doing here?"

"It belongs to the photographers and technicians."

"Oh, yes, fingerprints."

She would know about fingerprints, of course. She was always reading novels, detective stories among them, no doubt.

"Well, my dear Lucas?"

"Nothing much, Chief. As you thought, the fellow wore rubber gloves. All they could do was to make casts of his footprints. He was wearing brand-new shoes. Probably hadn't had them more than two or three days."

Félicie had gone up to her bedroom, to take off her veil and mourning garments.

"Have you any news, Chief? I get the feeling . . ."

He knew him so well. Maigret, in his present expansive and receptive mood, seemed to breathe life in at every pore. He looked about him. These surroundings, which had become so familiar to him that, without realizing it, he was beginning to take on some of the mannerisms of the people who lived there . . .

"What would you say to a drink?"

He went to the sideboard in the dining room, got out the

bottle of brandy, which was not quite empty, filled two little glasses, and went and stood in the doorway, looking out into the garden.

"Cheers! Félicie, my dear, I wonder . . ."

She had reappeared, wearing an apron, and was looking about her to make sure that the technicians from the Forensic Laboratory had not messed up her kitchen.

"I wonder if you would be so kind as to make a cup of coffee for my friend Lucas? I have business at the Anneau d'Or myself, but the Sergeant will take good care of you. See you this evening."

She gave him a look of mingled anxiety and mistrust, as was only to be expected.

"I really am going to the Anneau d'Or, I promise you."

And so he was, but not for long. Since there was no taxi to be had in Orgeval, he asked Louvet, the mechanic, to drive him to Paris in his truck.

"To Place des Ternes, please . . . The best way is via Rue du Faubourg-Saint-Honoré."

When he got there, he found the restaurant deserted. The waiter must have been having a nap somewhere behind the scenes, because, when he finally appeared, his hair was standing up in spikes and he was yawning.

"Do you happen to know the home address of the gentleman who was lunching here today, and to whom you gave a note from the lady who was with me?"

The silly fool, mistaking Maigret for a jealous lover or a possessive father, denied having done any such thing. The Chief Superintendent produced his card.

"Honest to God, I don't know his name. I don't think he lives around here, because he only ever comes in for lunch. . . ."

Maigret was not prepared to wait another day.

"Do you know where he works?"

"Let me think. . . . I seem to remember hearing him say

something about it to the boss. . . . I'll just go and see if he's in."

The waiter, it seemed, was not the only one to have been taking a nap. The proprietor appeared without a collar and smoothing his rumpled hair.

"Number 13? He's in leather goods. . . . He mentioned it one day, I remember, when we were chatting about this and that. . . . He works for a firm on Avenue de Wagram."

It did not take the Chief Superintendent long to locate the firm by means of the classified directory: Gellet and Mautoison, leather goods, import and export, 17B Avenue de Wagram. He went straight there. The offices were dark, with greenish windows, on which the name of the firm could be read backward, as in a mirror. He could hear the chatter of typewriters.

"The man you want to see is Monsieur Charles. . . . Just a minute . . ."

He was conducted through a maze of corridors and staircases smelling of animal skins to a little cubbyhole right at the back of the building, with a plate inscribed STATIONERY affixed to the door.

The man was Number 13, all right, looking grayer than ever in the long gray coverall he wore at work. The appearance of Maigret in his little sanctum gave him a considerable start.

"Sir?"

"I am from the Police Judiciaire. . . . You have nothing to fear. . . . I am merely seeking information."

"I don't see . . ."

"Oh, yes, you do, Monsieur Charles. You see very well. Be so good as to show me the note handed to you by the waiter in the restaurant earlier today."

"I swear to you . . ."

"I wouldn't do that if I were you, unless you want me to arrest you as an accessory to murder."

89

The man blew his nose noisily, not merely to gain time, but because he had a permanent cold in the head, which explained the heavy overcoat and muffler.

"You put me in a very awkward position."

"Not nearly as awkward as if you refuse to answer my questions."

Maigret had assumed his most hectoring tone. He was playing it rough, as Madame Maigret would have said. It always made her smile, knowing, as she alone did, what he was really like inside.

"Look here, Chief Superintendent, I had no idea . . ."

"To begin with, I want to see that note."

Instead of feeling for it in his pockets, as might have been expected, the man climbed a ladder and reached up to the very top shelf, where he had hidden it behind a stack of letterhead. He produced not only the note but also a revolver, which he handled gingerly, like someone terrified of firearms.

"For heaven's sake, whatever happens, say nothing. Throw you-know-what into the Seine. *It is a matter of life and death.*"

Maigret smiled at the last words, which were Félicie all over. Had she not said the same thing to Louvet, the mechanic from Orgeval?

"When I realized . . ."

"When you realized that someone had planted a revolver in your coat pocket—is that what you were going to say?"

"You knew about it?"

"You had just entered the Métro. In the crush, you were jostled by a young woman dressed in deep mourning, and you realized, as she made off toward the exit, that she had slipped something heavy into your pocket. . . ."

"It wasn't until later that I realized . . ."

"And you were very much alarmed. . . ."

"I've never handled a gun in my life. I couldn't even tell if it was loaded. I still don't know. . . ."

To the utter horror of the stationery clerk, Maigret removed the clip, from which one bullet was missing.

"But because there was something about that young woman in deep mourning . . ."

"I had every intention, at first, of handing in this . . . this object to the police. . . ."

Number 13 was looking distressed.

"You're a sensitive man, Monsieur Charles. You have a somewhat romantic view of women, have you not? I don't imagine you have had many amorous adventures in your life. . . ."

The sound of a bell. The poor man, terrified, looked up at a board above his desk.

"That's the boss wanting me. May I . . . ?"

"Run along! You've told me all I wanted to know."

"But that young lady . . . tell me . . . did she really . . . ?"

Maigret's brow darkened.

"As to that, only time will tell, Monsieur Charles. . . . Hurry, now. It wouldn't do to keep the boss waiting."

For the bell was ringing again, with imperious insistence.

Presently, having hailed a taxi in the street, the Chief Superintendent instructed the driver to take him to Gastinne-Renette, the gunsmith.

So, for three whole days, Félicie, well aware that she herself was under surveillance, and that every inch of the house and garden was likely to be searched, had kept the gun hidden on her person. He could just see her sitting beside the driver of the truck, realizing that there were too many cars around, and that the truck was possibly being followed. If she were to throw the gun out, Louvet might see her doing it. In Paris . . .

From the time she got out at Porte Maillot, she was aware that there was an inspector following her. To give herself time to think, she went into a patisserie and stuffed herself with cream puffs. She drank a glass of port. Possibly she didn't much care for port, but it represented gracious living to her, like the grapes and champagne that she had taken to the hospital. The Métro . . . There were too few people about at that time of day. She waited. The Inspector waited also, never taking his eyes off her.

Six o'clock, at long last. Crowds jostling on all the platforms, a solid mass of people. And one of them, providentially, wearing an overcoat with gaping pockets.

It was a pity that Félicie was not there to see Maigret as the taxi drove him to the gunsmith's. If she had been, self-satisfaction might well have triumphed over misery for a few seconds at the expression of admiration on the Chief Superintendent's face.

6

Maigret Stays Put

How many thousands of times had Maigret, with heavy tread, climbed the wide, dusty staircase of Police Headquarters, the steps always creaking a little underfoot, and, in winter, an icy draft swirling in the air? Maigret was a creature of habit. For instance, when he was almost at the top, he would invariably glance over his shoulder at the stairwell below. Invariably, also, when he reached the vast corridor of the floor occupied by the Police Judiciaire, he would stand for a moment gazing absently into the room generally known as the "aquarium." This room, immediately to the left of the staircase, was none other than the glass-walled waiting room, with its table covered in green baize, its chairs upholstered in green, and its walls hung with black frames, filled with small disk-shaped photographs of policemen killed in the line of duty.

Today, although it was already half past five, the waiting room was crowded. Maigret was so wrapped up in his own thoughts that he did not realize at first that most of these people were here at his behest. There were several familiar faces among them. One man sprang to his feet and accosted him:

"I say, Chief Superintendent, how much longer are we to

be kept waiting? You wouldn't consider seeing me first, as a personal favor, would you?"

All the craziest characters of Place Pigalle were there, rounded up, on his orders, by one of his inspectors.

"You know me, don't you? You know I'm on the level. I wouldn't dream of getting mixed up in a sordid business like that. I've been kicking my heels here all afternoon. . . ."

Maigret's broad back receded. Seemingly at random, he put his head around two or three of the office doorways that lined the corridor as far as the eye could see. The whole department was seething with activity. It was all so familiar to him. People were being interrogated all over the place, even in his own office, where Rondonnet, a recent addition to his staff, was sitting in Maigret's personal chair, and smoking a pipe just like the Chief's. In his eagerness to emulate Maigret, he had gone even further, and ordered glasses of beer to be sent across from the Brasserie Dauphine. In the chair opposite sat one of the waiters from the Pélican. Rondonnet winked at the Chief and, temporarily leaving his "patient" to his own devices, went out with him into the corridor, where such private interchanges so often took place.

"There's something in the wind, all right, Chief. I'm not quite sure what, yet. . . . You know how these things go. . . . I deliberately left them to stew in the aquarium. . . . Word has got around. One can feel it. They know something. . . . Have you seen the Chief Commissioner? Apparently he's been calling around, trying to get hold of you, for the last hour. Oh, and by the way . . . there's a message for you."

He went to fetch it from Maigret's desk. It was from Madame Maigret.

"Elise has arrived from Epinal with her husand and the children. I've asked them all to stay to dinner. I do hope you'll be able to join us. They've brought us some *cèpes.*"

Maigret would not be joining them. He had too much on

his mind. There was something he wanted to check, an idea that had occurred to him a short time ago, while he was waiting at the gunsmith's for Monsieur Gastinne-Renette's ballistics report. He had been pacing up and down in the shooting gallery in the basement, idly watching a young married couple, who were about to leave for Africa on their honeymoon, trying out some extremely powerful guns.

His thoughts, as usual, had returned to Peg Leg's cottage. Once again, he saw himself climbing the gleaming stairs, and then suddenly—the picture was absolutely clear in his mind— he saw himself hesitating on the landing, looking from one door to the other. And then he remembered the three bedrooms.

"Well, I'll be damned!"

And from then on, he had only one thought: to get back there as soon as possible, to confirm what he felt to be virtually a certainty. As to the ballistics report, he knew in advance what it would contain, for there was no doubt in his mind that the revolver recovered on Avenue de Wagram was the one used in the killing of old Lapie. A Smith & Wesson. Not a toy, by any means. Not the sort of weapon favored by amateurs, but the real thing, a professional killer's gun.

A quarter of an hour later, old Monsieur Gastinne-Renette confirmed his theory.

"You were right, Chief Superintendent. It is the same gun. I'll send you my detailed written report tonight, with the enlarged photographs."

Maigret had decided, nevertheless, to look in at the Quai, to find out if there had been any new developments. He was now standing outside the Chief Commissioner's padded door. He knocked.

"Ah! There you are, Maigret! I was afraid you might not get my message. Was it you who sent Dunan to Rue Lepic?"

Maigret had forgotten all about it, but yes, he had. Just

on the off chance. He had instructed Dunan to make a thorough search of the room Jacques Pétillon had occupied in the Hotel Beauséjour.

"He telephoned in a short time ago. It seems someone had been there before him. He'd like a word with you as soon as possible. Will you be going there?"

He nodded, feeling gloomy and oppressed. He hated having his train of thought interrupted, and his mind was filled with Jeanneville, not with Rue Lepic.

As he was leaving the building, he was stopped in his tracks by another of the characters who had been rounded up and left to stew in the aquarium.

"Could you possibly arrange for me to be seen right away? I have a pile of things to attend to. . . ."

He shrugged. A little later, as he got out of his taxi in Place Blanche, he felt suddenly dizzy. The whole square was bathed in sunlight. The wide terrace of one of the big cafés was crowded with people, as if there were nothing more to life than sitting at a table, drinking a cold beer or an apéritif, and ogling the pretty women as they went by.

Maigret experienced a fleeting pang of envy. He thought of his wife, who, at this very moment, was entertaining her sister and brother-in-law in their apartment on Boulevard Richard-Lenoir. He thought of the *cèpes,* simmering on the stove, and exuding an appetizing smell of garlic and damp woodland. He adored *cèpes.*

He wished he had the leisure to join the throng on the terrace. It was several days since he had last had a decent night's sleep, and he had eaten nothing but odd snacks, with a snatched drink here and there of whatever he could get. It seemed to him that he was compelled, by virtue of his wretched calling, to live the lives of a whole lot of other people, instead of quietly getting on with his own. Oh, well, thank goodness, he would be retiring in a few years' time, and then, with a broad-brimmed straw hat on his head, he would cultivate his garden, a carefully tended garden like old Lapie's, and, like Lapie, he would resort to the cellar, from time to time, for a refreshing glass of wine.

"Bring me a small beer . . . and hurry."

He had barely had time to sit down when he caught sight of Inspector Dunan, who had been watching for him.

"I was hoping you'd come, Chief. . . . Wait till you see . . ."

Away in Jeanneville, Félicie would be busy cooking her evening meal on the gas stove, with the kitchen door wide open, and the kitchen garden bathed in the golden glow of the setting sun.

The Hotel Beauséjour was wedged between a shoeshop and a pork butcher's. They went in. At the reception desk, which was glassed in, a monstrously fat man sat in a high-backed chair, with his grossly swollen feet immersed in an enamel basin of water. Beside him was a wooden panel, on which hung the keys of the bedrooms.

"I assure you, I am not to blame. You have only to ask Ernest. He was the one who showed them upstairs. . . ."

Ernest, the porter, who looked even sleepier than Maigret, because he was on duty night and day and seldom managed to snatch more than two hours' sleep at a stretch, explained in a drowsy voice:

"It was early this afternoon. . . . At that time of day, we get no one in but *casuals*, if you get my meaning. That's all the rooms on the first floor are used for. . . . The women are mostly regulars. . . . They usually just call out on their way up:

" 'I'm going up to Number 8,' or whatever.

"And when they come down again, they collect their commission. . . . They get five francs a time, you understand.

"I mentioned at the time that I didn't recognize that one. . . . A dark girl, rather less shopworn than most of

97

them . . . She waited here in the lobby to be given a key."

"What about the man with her?" asked Maigret.

"I couldn't say. . . . We never look at them too closely, you know, because they don't like it. It embarrasses them. Some deliberately turn their backs, or pretend to blow their noses, and in winter they wear their coat collars turned up. . . . He was just a man like any other. I didn't notice anything special about him. . . . I took them up to Number 5, which happened to be available at the time. . . ."

A couple came up to the desk. The girl asked:

"Is Number 9 free, Ernest?"

The bloated old man glanced at the board, and replied with a nod and a grunt.

"That's Jaja. . . . She's one of the regulars, all right! What was I saying? Oh, yes . . . The man came down first, after about a quarter of an hour. . . . That's the usual thing. .·. . I didn't see the woman leave. But anyway, about ten minutes later I went up to the room, found it empty, and tidied up.

"I must have missed her as she went out, I said to myself.

"Then things got busy, and I forgot all about it, and it must have been half an hour later or more when, to my amazement, I caught sight of the woman slinking out behind my back. . . .

"That's odd! I said to myself. Where has she been hiding?

"After that, I didn't give it another thought until your inspector, who had borrowed the key to the saxophone player's room, came down again and started asking questions."

"You say you'd never seen her before?"

"No . . . I couldn't say that. All I know for sure is that she wasn't a regular. . . . And yet there was something vaguely familiar about her. . . . I had the feeling that I had seen her somewhere before."

"How long have you been working here?"

"Five years."

"So you might possibly have seen her here sometime in the past?"

"It's possible. . . . We get so many of them in and out, you know. They turn up regularly for a time, a fortnight or a month, perhaps, and then they move to some other district, or to the provinces, or get pulled in by your fellows. . . ."

With heavy tread, Maigret went upstairs with the Inspector. Pétillon's room was high up, on the fifth floor. The lock had not been forced. It was a very ordinary lock, and could have been opened with the commonest type of passkey.

Maigret looked about him and whistled, for whoever had ransacked the room had certainly made a good job of it. There was not much furniture, but what there was had been turned inside out. Pétillon's gray suit was lying on the rug with the pockets hanging out. All the drawers were open, and their contents scattered about. To top it all, the young woman had slit open the mattress, the pillow, and the eiderdown with a pair of scissors, and the floor was covered in a snowdrift of down and wadding.

"What do you make of it, Chief?"

"Any fingerprints?"

"The people from Criminal Records have already been. I took the liberty of calling them myself. They sent along Moers, but he didn't find anything. What on earth could they have been looking for, to turn the place upside down like this?"

That was not what interested Maigret. What they had been looking for, as Dunan put it, suggesting that there was more than one person involved, was far less significant than the thoroughness and determination of the search. And, what was more, there had not been a single blunder!

The revolver that had killed Jules Lapie was a Smith & Wesson, a weapon favored by the hard core of the criminal fraternity.

What had been the sequence of events following the old

man's death? Pétillon had lost his head. He had dashed madly from one sleazy Montmartre dive to another, in search of someone who was not to be found. Even the knowledge that the police were after him had not stopped him. He had pressed on with his search, traveling all the way to Rouen to inquire for a girl named Adèle, who had worked at the Tivoli brasserie until a few months before.

It was at this point that he had visibly lost heart. He had reached the end of his rope. He had given up the struggle. Maigret had only to pick him up, and he would talk.

And it was then that he was shot full in the chest, right out in the open, in the middle of a busy street. One thing was certain: his assailant was no novice at the game.

Surely it was this same man who, wasting no time, had made straight for Jeanneville?

In Place Pigalle, Pétillon had been accompanied by no less a person than the Chief Superintendent himself, but that had not deterred his would-be murderer.

Lapie's house had been under constant surveillance. The man must have been aware of this, or at least suspected it, but, still undeterred, he had broken into the bedroom, pushed a chair up against the wardrobe, and wrenched off one of the planks at the top.

Had he found what he was looking for? Interrupted by Félicie, he had knocked her down and fled, leaving no traces other than a few unhelpful footprints, made by brand-new shoes.

This last incident had taken place between three and four in the morning, and already, by this afternoon, Pétillon's room had been ransacked.

This time, the culprit was a woman. A dark, reasonably attractive woman, like Adèle from the brasserie in Rouen. She had not slipped up in any way. According to the hall porter, the renting of rooms by the hour for the purposes of prostitu-

100

tion was so commonplace that if she had brought an accomplice in with her instead of a client, no one would have noticed. But she could not be sure that the Hotel Beauséjour was not also under surveillance. So she decided to play it straight. She picked up a man in the usual way, and requested the use of a room. But, when he had left, instead of going out after him, she had slunk upstairs to the fifth floor, knowing that the upper floors were deserted at that time of day, and searched every inch of the room.

What conclusion was to be drawn from this ever more rapid succession of events? That time was running out for *them*. That *they* had to find what they were looking for in the shortest possible time. It therefore followed that whatever it was, *they* had not yet found it.

And, on this account, Maigret, too, was seized with a feverish sense that time was running out. It was a feeling that seemed to overwhelm him every time he abandoned his surveillance of Cape Horn. It was as if he had some premonition of disaster.

He snapped back the elastic band of his notebook, scribbled a note, and tore out the page. It read:

Institute exhaustive search of the Ninth and Eighteenth Arrondissements tonight.

"Take this to Superintendent Piaulet. He will understand."

Out in the street once more, his glance returned to the café terrace, crowded with people who had nothing to do but enjoy themselves and savor the spring weather. What the hell! Surely there was time for another quick beer? With froth still clinging to his trim mustache, he bundled into a taxi and sat slumped in his seat.

"First, take me to Poissy. . . . I'll give you directions from there."

Manfully, he struggled against waves of drowsiness. With

101

half-closed eyes, he promised himself that as soon as this case was over he would sleep for twenty-four hours at a stretch. He could picture his bedroom, with the windows wide open, and the sunlight flickering on the counterpane, the familiar sounds of home, Madame Maigret tiptoeing about, and shushing the delivery boys if they made too much noise.

But, as the popular song has it, that day would never come. It was just a dream, an empty promise, a hollow resolution. When the time came, the wretched telephone would ring, that telephone that Madame Maigret always longed to stifle with a pillow, as if it were some malevolent living thing.

"Hello. Yes . . ."

And Maigret would be off on his travels again.

"Where to now, sir?"

"Turn left up the hill. . . . I'll tell you when to stop."

Drowsy as he was, he was nevertheless impatient of delay. The thought had occurred to him at the gunsmith's, and he had been obsessed with it ever since. Why had it not struck him sooner? Still, he felt he had finally hit the jackpot, as they say in gambling circles. From the start, he had been intrigued by the layout of the three bedrooms. And then he had allowed himself to be led astray by notions of the old man's jealous disposition.

"It's on the right. . . . Yes . . . The third cottage . . . Look here, I've half a mind to keep you here for the night. . . . Have you had dinner? No? Hold on . . . Lucas! Come over here a minute, old fellow. . . . Any new developments? Is Félicie here? . . . What's that? She invited you in for a cup of coffee and a drop of brandy? . . . No, no! You're wrong about that. It's not because she's scared. It's because I told off a pert little hospital nurse this morning for making fun of her. She's showing her gratitude to me by being decent to you, that's all. . . . Make the most of it while you can. . . . Be off with you now to the Anneau d'Or. . . . Have some dinner, and see that

102

the driver does, too. . . . Keep in touch with the postmistress. I've warned her to expect calls all through the night. . . . Is my bike here?"

"It's in the garden, propped up against the wall of the cellar."

Félicie was standing in the doorway, watching them. When the car drove off, Maigret went toward her, and saw that she was, once again, bristling with mistrust.

"So you went back to Paris, *in spite of everything?*"

He knew what she was thinking. Had he gone back to the little restaurant where they had had lunch, and found the gentleman with the overcoat and muffler, and had he talked, in spite of her pathetic little note?

"Come with me, Félicie. This is no time for playing games."

"Where are you going?"

"Upstairs . . . Come along."

He opened the door of old Lapie's bedroom.

"Now, I want you to think carefully. . . . Jacques spent several months in this room, if I'm not mistaken. . . . Can you tell me exactly how the room was furnished at that time?"

The question took her by surprise. She looked around, trying to remember.

"To begin with, there was the brass bed, which is now in the storeroom—at least that's what I call it. . . . It's the room next to mine, which I slept in for several months. . . . Since then, it's been used for storing all the old junk in the house, and the apples are stored there in the autumn."

"The bed . . . That's one thing. . . . And what else? What about the dressing table?"

"No, it's the same one."

"What about chairs?"

"Let me think. There were a couple of chairs with leather seats. . . . They're in the dining room now. . . ."

"And the wardrobe?"

He had deliberately left it till last, and he was so tense that he bit right through the ebonite mouthpiece of his pipe.

"It's the same one."

It was a fearful letdown. He had hurried back all the way from Paris, only to find that he was up against a brick wall, or, even worse, a gaping void.

"No, I'm wrong. . . . It was the same as this, but not the same one. There are two of these wardrobes, exactly alike, in the house. He bought them at an auction three or four years ago. I can't remember exactly when. . . . I was a bit upset about it, because I wanted a wardrobe with a mirror. There isn't a single full-length mirror in the house. . . ."

Phew! If she only knew what a load she had just taken off his mind! Leaving her standing, almost forgetting her existence, he ran headlong into Félicie's bedroom, and through to the adjoining room, where he opened the window and flung back the wooden shutters with a clatter.

Why had he not thought of it sooner? The room was crammed with stuff, a roll of linoleum, old rugs, chairs stacked one on top of the other, as in a café after closing time. There were unpainted deal shelves, used, no doubt, for storing apples in winter, an old pump in a crate, two tables, and finally, right at the back, behind all this bric-à-brac, a wardrobe identical with the one in the old man's bedroom.

Maigret was in such a hurry that he knocked over the dismantled sections of the brass bedstead, which were stacked against the wall. He pushed one of the tables up against the wardrobe, climbed onto it, and felt along the dusty boards behind the cornice.

"Could you get me some sort of tool?"

"What kind of tool?"

"A screwdriver, scissors, pliers, anything . . ."

The dust drifted down on his hair like powder. Félicie had

104

gone downstairs. He could hear her footsteps on the garden path. She went into the cellar, and returned at long last with a hammer and chisel.

"What are you going to do?"

Pry up the boards, of course, what else? And besides, it was easy enough. One of them was loose already. Underneath it, Maigret felt a wad of paper. He pulled out what proved to be a small package wrapped in an old newspaper.

He looked at Félicie, whose face was lifted up to his. She was pale and tense.

"What's in this parcel?"

"I haven't the remotest idea."

Her voice had the old, familiar sharp edge; her expression was defiant.

He climbed down from the table.

"We'll soon find out, won't we? Are you sure you don't know what's in it?"

Did he believe her, or did he not? He seemed to be playing cat and mouse. He took his time, subjecting her to a long look, before unwrapping the parcel.

"The newspaper is more than a year old. . . . Well, well! Félicie, my dear, did you know that there was a fortune hidden in the house?"

For the parcel that he had just opened contained a thick wad of thousand-franc notes.

"Careful! Don't touch!"

He climbed back onto the table and loosened all the other boards on top of the wardrobe, to make sure that nothing else was hidden there.

"We'll be more comfortable downstairs. Come along. . . ."

Feeling very pleased with himself, he sat down at the kitchen table. Maigret had always had a weakness for kitchens, with their appetizing smells and piles of good things to eat, plump vegetables, juicy meat, poultry waiting to be plucked.

105

The half-bottle of brandy from which Félicie had poured a glass for Lucas was still there, and he helped himself to a drop or two before settling down to count the money, which he did conscientiously, like a professional cashier.

"Two hundred and ten . . . eleven . . . twelve . . . Wait a minute, there are two stuck together here. . . . Thirteen, fourteen . . . Two hundred and twenty-three, four . . . seven, eight . . ."

He looked at her. She was staring fixedly at the notes, her face drained of color, so that the bruises she had received the night before stood out in sharp contrast.

"Two hundred and twenty-nine thousand francs, Félicie, my love . . . What do you say to that? There were two hundred and twenty-nine thousand-franc notes hidden in your little friend Pétillon's bedroom. . . .

"Because that, undoubtedly, is where the money was hidden, don't you see? The gentleman who is at present so urgently in need of money knew exactly where to look. . . . There was just one thing he didn't know, which was that there were two identical wardrobes in the house. . . . And, anyway, even if he had known, it would never have occurred to him that Lapie was such an old fusspot that when he moved back into his own room, he would insist on taking his own wardrobe with him."

"Where does that get you?" she said, in a strained voice.

"Well, for one thing, it explains why you were knocked down last night, and also why, a few hours later, your friend Jacques's hotel bedroom on Rue Lepic was ransacked. . . ."

He stood up. He needed to stretch his legs. He was not entirely happy. To have achieved one object was not enough. Now that he had found what he had been looking for, and been vindicated by the results—he had a vivid mental picture of Gastinne-Renette's shooting gallery, where the notion had suddenly struck him—now that he had resolved one problem,

106

others were coming to the fore. He paced up and down the garden, straightened the bent stem of a rose bush, and absently picked up the seeder which Lapie, better known as Peg Leg, had dropped a few minutes before going meekly upstairs to his bedroom to die.

Through the open window the Chief Superintendent could see Félicie standing motionless as a statue. A faint smile played about his lips. And why not? He shrugged, as if to say:

"Well, there's no harm in trying!"

And, fidgeting with the seeder, to which lumps of soil were still clinging, he spoke to her through the window:

"You see, child, I am becoming more and more convinced that, strange as it may seem to you, Jacques Pétillon did not kill his uncle. I'll go further, and say that I don't believe he played any significant part in the whole dreadful business."

She looked at him, but did not stir. He could see not the slightest tremor of relief on her drawn features.

"What do you say to that? You must be pleased, surely?"

She forced herself to smile, but it was a pathetic effort, no more than a slight twitching of her thin lips.

"I am pleased. Thank you."

He was in an ebullient mood, but with an effort was able to restrain himself.

"I can see you're pleased, very pleased. And I'm sure that now you will do everything you can to help me prove the innocence of the boy you love. . . . You do love him, don't you?"

She turned her head away, doubtless so that he would not see her quivering mouth and tear-filled eyes.

"Come now, of course you love him. There's nothing to be ashamed of in that. I'm sure he's going to pull through, and when he does, he'll receive you with open arms, in gratitude for all you've done for him."

"I haven't done anything for him."

"Well, let that pass. . . . It doesn't matter. I still say I'm convinced you'll marry him, and have lots of children."

As he had expected, she blew up. Was not this precisely what he had been aiming at?

"You're a brute! A brute! You're the cruelest, the most . . . the most . . ."

"Because I tell you that Jacques is innocent?"

Those few simple words got through to her at last, in the very midst of her outburst of rage. She knew that she was in the wrong, but it was too late. She did not know what to say; she was miserable and, at the same time, utterly at sea.

"You know very well you don't believe that. . . . It's just a trick to make me talk. . . . From the very first moment you set foot in this house . . ."

"When was the last time you saw Pétillon?"

Her presence of mind had not wholly deserted her.

"This morning," she quickly retorted.

"Before that, I mean."

She did not reply, and Maigret ostentatiously turned his back on her, gazing across the garden at the summerhouse, where, on that fateful morning, a half-bottle of brandy and two glasses had been set out on the green table. Her eyes followed his gaze. She knew what he was thinking.

"I'm not saying anything."

"I know. You have already told me so at least twenty times. It's beginning to sound like the chorus of a song. . . . It's lucky for us that we found the money."

"What do you mean?"

"Oh, so you are interested, after all? When Pétillon left Cape Horn, a year ago, it was because he had quarreled with his uncle—isn't that so?"

"They didn't get on, but . . ."

"So, after that, he never came back. . . ."

She was trying to figure out what he was getting at now. Her face was working with the effort.

"And you never saw him again!" said Maigret at last. "Or, rather, you never saw him to speak to again. If you had, you would no doubt have told him that the wardrobes had been switched."

She was quick to sense the danger in these insidious questions and statements. Good heavens, how could a defenseless girl hope to outwit this imperturbable man, standing there smoking his pipe and beaming at her like an indulgent father? She hated him. Yes, she hated him. Never in all her life had she been made to suffer as this Chief Superintendent had made her suffer, not allowing her a moment's peace, puffing away at his pipe, and making the most disconcerting remarks as casually as if he were passing the time of day.

"You were never his mistress, Félicie?"

Ought she to say yes? Ought she to say no? What was all this leading up to?

"If you had been his mistress, you and he would have gone on meeting, because the row with his uncle had nothing to do with your relationship. You would have had plenty of opportunities to tell him about the old man moving back to his own room. Pétillon would have known that the money was no longer there, but in the storeroom. You see what I'm getting at? Knowing that, he would have had no occasion to go into his uncle's bedroom, and there, for whatever reason, kill the old man. . . ."

"It's not true. . . ."

"So you were not his mistress."

"No."

"Was there ever anything at all between you?"

"No."

"In other words, he didn't know you were in love with him?"

109

"That's right."

A complacent smile spread over Maigret's features.

"Well, my dear, I do believe that, at last, for the first time since the beginning of this case, you are telling the truth. . . . As to your feelings for the boy, I was never in any doubt. I knew all about that right from the start. . . . You've never had much fun out of life, my poor child. So, having little that was real to draw on, you lived in a world of dreams. You saw yourself not as little Félicie, old Monsieur Lapie's servant girl, but as all the glamorous heroines of romantic fiction rolled into one.

"In your dream world, Peg Leg was no longer your cantankerous employer, but, as in all the best popular novels, your natural father. There's no need to blush. You had to have a romantic history, if only for something to tell your friend Léontine, and to write in your diary.

"The first man to cross the threshold of this house was transformed in your imagination into your lover. It was the grand romantic passion, though I'm as sure as I am of anything that the poor boy hadn't an inkling of what was going on in your mind. I am equally sure that the manager of this development, Forrentin, never made a pass at you, but that, on account of his goaty beard, you transformed him into a satyr."

As he said this, a fleeting smile played about Félicie's lips. But it was soon gone, to be replaced by her customary hostile expression.

"What is all this leading up to?"

"I don't know yet," he admitted, "but I soon will, thanks to the money we've found. Now, I'm going to ask you a favor. The people who are searching for that money, and who need it so desperately that they are prepared to take such risks as they have done in the past few days, are not likely to give up at this late stage. . . . The simple idea that occurred to me, that there were two identical wardrobes and that they had been

110

switched, could also occur to them. . . . I would be much easier in my mind if I knew that you were not going to be left all alone here tonight. I know you hate me, but even so, I'd be obliged if you would agree to my spending the night here. You can lock your bedroom door. What have you got for dinner?"

"Blood sausage, and I was thinking of making mashed potatoes to go with it."

"Splendid. May I invite myself to dinner? I just have to pop over to Orgeval to see to a couple of things, and then I'll be back. Agreed?"

"Whatever you say."

"Come on, now, let me see you smile."

"No . . ."

He stuffed the bank notes into his pocket and went to fetch his bicycle, which was propped up against the cellar wall. While he was there, he thought he might as well pour himself a glass of wine. Having drunk it, he mounted the bicycle, and was just about to ride off, when she called out to him.

"Just the same, I still hate you!"

Turning around with a beaming smile, he retorted:

"And I, my dear Félicie, adore you!"

7

A Lobster Dinner

Half past six in the evening. That was about the time when Maigret, astride his bicycle outside Cape Horn, had turned around to call out to Félicie, standing in the cottage doorway:

"And I adore you!"

At Béziers, the telephone was ringing in the Superintendent's office at Police Headquarters. The window was wide open. The office was empty. Arsène Vadibert, the Superintendent's secretary, was watching a game of bowls in his shirt sleeves under the plane trees. He turned toward the barred window, through which the shrill, insistent ringing could be heard.

"Coming! Coming!" he called out, sounding more than a little reluctant. His thick, nasal regional accent was difficult to understand over the telephone.

"Coming! Coming! Hello! . . . Paris, did you say? . . . Eh? What? This is Béziers . . . Béziers, yes, spelled as it's pronounced. The Police Judiciaire? . . . We received your note. . . . I said your *nottttte*. Don't you people in Paris understand French? . . . Your note on the subject of a girl named Adèle . . . Well, I think we may have something for you."

He leaned forward a little to watch Grêlé, wearing a white shirt, crouching in preparation for a spectacular throw.

"It happened last week—Thursday it was—in the *maison.*" (Needless to say, he pronounced it *maisong.*) . . . "What did you say? . . . Which *maisong*? . . . *The maisong,* of course . . . The one here is called the Paradon. . . . A girl by the name of Adèle . . . a little, dark girl . . . What? . . . Pear-shaped breasts? . . . As to that, *mossieu,* I couldn't say; I've never seen her breasts. . . . And besides, she's run off. . . . If you'd only listen, you'd know the answer to that. . . . I have enough on my plate already. . . . As I was saying, this girl Adèle decided to move out, and asked to be paid off. The assistant manageress sent for the proprietor. Apparently she wasn't entitled to leave just like that. She had to give a month's notice. Anyway, he refused to give her the money owing to her, and she went berserk, and started smashing bottles and ripping up cushions. There was a hell of a rumpus, but in the end she left anyway, though, not having a sou to bless herself with, she had to borrow some money from one of the other girls. . . . She was bound for Paris. . . . What? . . . I haven't the vaguest idea. . . . You asked for an Adèle, and I've given you one. . . . So long, chum . . ."

Thirty-five minutes past six. The Anneau d'Or in Orgeval. A grayish-white façade with an open door in the middle. A bench on either side of the door. At the end of each bench, a bay tree in a tub. Benches and tubs painted dark green. Half the street sunlit, the other half in shadow. A truck drew up outside the inn, and the butcher got out, wearing a blue-and-white-checked coverall.

In the bar, where it was cool and dark, the landlord, Forrentin, Lepape, and the driver of Maigret's taxi were playing cards. Lucas stood watching them, nonchalantly smoking his pipe, his manner consciously modeled on that of the Chief Superintendent. The landlord's wife was rinsing glasses.

"Good evening, everybody!" called out the butcher. "A pint for me, Madame Jeanne . . . By the way, could you make

113

use of a fine lobster? I've just been given two in town, and I'm the only one at home who eats lobster, because my old woman claims it makes her break out in a rash."

He went out to fetch the live lobster from his truck, and returned carrying it by one claw. Across the way, a window was flung open, a hand was seen to wave, and a voice called out:

"Telephone, Monsieur Lucas."

"One minute, Monsieur Lucas, before you go. Do you like lobster?"

Did he like lobster!

"Germaine! Get a court bouillon ready, would you, as soon as you can. I have a lobster here, waiting to be cooked."

"Hello! Lucas speaking, yes . . . The Chief should be here any moment now. . . . What? From Béziers? Adèle? Thursday?"

Maigret arrived on his bicycle just as the butcher's truck drove off. Lucas was still on the telephone. He went into the bar and stood watching the cardplayers. The lobster was crawling about clumsily on the tiled floor near the bar counter.

"Tell me, madame, is that lobster yours? Could you bear to part with it, I wonder?"

"I was just about to cook it for your sergeant and the driver."

"They can make do with something else. If you don't mind, I'll take this back with me."

Lucas came across the road.

"I think they've found Adèle, Chief. . . . In Béziers . . . She left there suddenly for Paris on Thursday."

The cardplayers glanced at them every now and then, trying to catch what they were saying.

Ten minutes to seven. Inspector Rondonnet and Chief Superintendent Piaulet were talking in one of the offices of Police Headquarters. The high windows looked out on the

Seine, where a tug could be heard chugging wheezily.

"Hello! Is that Orgeval? . . . I'd be much obliged, mademoiselle, if you would call Chief Superintendent Maigret to speak to me."

The waving hand appeared once more at the window. Lucas ran across the street. Maigret, carrying the lobster, was just about to remount his bike.

"It's for you, Chief."

"Hello! Piaulet? Any developments?"

"Rondonnet thinks he may be on to something. According to the doorman of the Sancho, which is just opposite the Pélican, the proprietor of the Pélican was seen to make a phone call from the café on the corner last night while you were in his place. . . . Hello? . . . Yes . . . Not long after that, a taxi showed up. No one got out. The proprietor talked in a whisper to someone inside. . . . Do you see what I'm getting at? . . . Sounds fishy, don't you think? . . . And another thing: on Saturday night, there was a row in the tobacconist's on Rue Fontaine. It's hard to say, exactly. . . . The man involved wasn't a regular. . . ."

"Ouch!" exclaimed Maigret.

"What?"

"It's nothing. . . . Just the lobster . . . Go on."

"That's about all, really. . . . We're continuing the interrogations. . . . I have the feeling that some of them know a lot more than they're telling."

"All that can wait till I get back. . . . Hello? . . . By the way, I want some information from Criminal Records. . . . Something that happened about thirteen months ago—I'm not quite sure what. A holdup, maybe, or a case of fraud . . . I want to know whether any of the Place Pigalle fraternity was living with a girl named Adèle about that time. . . . Lucas will be within reach all night, so it doesn't matter how late you call back. . . . What's going on?"

"One moment . . . Rondonnet, who has been listening on the extension, wants to say something. I'll put him on."

"Hello, is that you, Chief? I don't know if it's of any significance, but I've suddenly remembered something. . . . Anyway, the date fits. . . . It happened in April of last year. . . . I was on the case myself. It was on Rue Blanche, remember? Pedro, the proprietor of the Chamois . . ."

Seeing that the lobster would not keep still, Maigret put it gently down on the floor, and growled:

"Don't move."

"What?"

"It's the lobster. . . . Pedro . . . No . . . Sorry, it doesn't ring a bell."

"He ran a small nightclub, not unlike the Pélican, but even sleazier, on Rue Blanche. . . . He was tall and thin, very pale, with a white streak, just one, in his black hair. . . ."

"I'm with you."

"It was three in the morning. He was just about to close when a car drew up, and five men got out, leaving the motor running. The headwaiter was already putting up the shutters. . . . They shoved him aside. . . ."

"I have a vague recollection of it."

"They bundled Pedro into a little back room behind the bar. A few minutes later, there was a volley of shots, and a lot of splintered glass and flying bottles. Then the whole place suddenly went dark. I happened to be in the neighborhood at the time. . . . By a miracle, we reached the spot in time to catch four of the villains, including the Fly, who had fled to the roof. . . . Pedro was dead, with five or six bullets in him. . . . Only one of the killers got away, and it took us several days to find out who he was. It was Albert Babeau, the Musician. The one they call Midget, because he really is undersized, and wears platform soles to increase his height. . . . Hold on. Piaulet is saying something. . . . No . . . He wants to speak to you."

116

"Hello, Maigret . . . I remember the case, too. . . . I have the file in my office. Would you like me to . . . ?"

"There's no need. It's all coming back to me. . . . The Musician was arrested at Le Havre, wasn't he? How long after the incident?"

"About a week . . . We got an anonymous tip."

"How many years did he get?"

"I'd have to look up his record for that. . . . The Fly was the one they came down on hardest, because three shots had been fired from his revolver. . . . Twenty years he got, if I'm not mistaken. The others got between one and five years. . . . Pedro was reputed to keep large sums of money on the premises, but nothing was found. . . . Do you think there could be any connection? . . . Look, couldn't you come and see me here, and we could talk it over?"

Maigret hesitated. His foot knocked against the lobster.

"I can't make it just now. . . . Listen . . . What needs to be done is this. Lucas will be on call all through the night. . . ."

As he came out of the phone booth, he remarked to the postmistress:

"I warned you that you probably wouldn't get much sleep tonight. It now looks as if you won't get any."

He had a brief word with Lucas, who eyed the lobster gloomily.

"Very good, Chief . . . I've got it, Chief. . . . What about the taxi?"

"Better keep it, for the time being."

The sky was splashed with the glorious colors of a splendid sunset as Maigret returned along the road he had taken so many times in the past few days. Affectionately, he contemplated the toy cottages of Jeanneville, knowing that, before long, this now familiar landscape would be nothing more than a memory.

The soil smelled good, the grass was lush, the crickets

were beginning to chirp, and, he thought, there was no sight on earth more soothing and innocent than a row of neatly tended vegetable gardens, with their owners, in straw hats, peaceably plying their hoses.

"It's I!" he called out, stepping into the hallway of Cape Horn, which was filled with the smell of frying blood sausage.

And, hiding the lobster behind his back:

"Tell me, Félicie . . . This is important, mind. . . ."

She was instantly on the defensive.

"Do you know how to make mayonnaise, at least?"

A disdainful smile.

"Very well, then, get on with it, and meanwhile put this gentleman here on to boil."

He was in high good humor. He rubbed his hands. Then, noticing that the dining-room door was open, he went in. The table, he saw, was laid for one, with a red-and-white-checked cloth, a glass, silver cutlery, and an attractively arranged basket of bread. He frowned, but said nothing.

He waited, little suspecting that this lobster, even now turning red in the pot of boiling water, was to be the subject of endless teasing by his wife. Madame Maigret was not of a jealous disposition, or so she claimed.

"Jealous of what, for heaven's sake?" she would often exclaim, with a little forced laugh.

Which did not prevent her from seizing every opportunity, when the subject of Maigret's work came up among relations or friends, of saying:

"It's not all hard work, you know. It has its compensations. One might, for instance, in the course of an inquiry, find oneself dining on lobster with a girl named Félicie, and spending the night with her afterward. . . ."

Poor Félicie! Good heavens, the last thing on her mind was an amorous adventure! As she came and went, her stubborn Norman mind, behind that bulging nanny-goat forehead

118

of hers, was filled with anxious, if not desperate, thoughts. The coming of dusk brought her only deepening sadness and uneasiness. Through the open window, she watched Maigret pacing back and forth. Perhaps she, like Our Lord, was wondering whether this cup would ever be taken from her.

He had picked a bunch of flowers and was arranging them in a vase.

"By the way, Félicie, where did poor old Lapie have his meals?"

"In the kitchen. Why? It wasn't worth messing up the dining room, just for him alone."

"Indeed!"

And there he was, scooping up the cutlery and the cloth, and setting a place for himself at the table near the stove, while she stirred the mayonnaise feverishly, convinced that it was about to curdle.

"If all goes well, and if you behave yourself, I may have some good news for you tomorrow morning."

"What news?"

"How can I tell you, since I won't know until the morning?"

Anxious though he might be to spare her feelings, he could not help himself.

He knew that she was unhappy and distraught, and strained almost to the breaking point, and yet he could not refrain from teasing her. It was as if he felt impelled to get back at her in some way.

Was it perhaps because he had a slightly guilty conscience about being here instead of in Paris, conducting operations in preparation for the grand climax that was building up around and about Place Pigalle?

"The front line is no place for a general."

True enough. But ought he to be skulking quite so far in the rear, with a chain of messages buzzing to and fro, keeping the postmistress up all night, and making that good fellow Lucas trot back and forth between Orgeval and Jeanneville as if he were nothing better than a village postman?

The man who broke in, looking for the money, might think of the changing around of the furniture and come back. And this time, he might do worse than merely stun Félicie with a blow of his fist.

All of which, needless to say, was perfectly true. Still, it was not Maigret's real reason for staying. If the truth were told, he had stayed because he liked it here. It was so peaceful in this comic little fairy-tale village, even though, all the while, he was directing operations in another far-off, much more real and violent world.

"Why have you brought all that stuff in here?"

"Because I want us to have dinner together. . . . I said so, remember, when I invited myself. This is the first and probably the last meal we shall be sharing, unless . . ."

He smiled.

"Unless what?" she asked.

"Nothing. You will hear all about it tomorrow morning, child, and then, if we have time, we can also add up all the lies you've told me. . . . Here, have this claw. . . . Yes, I insist. . . ."

And, all of a sudden, as he was eating under the ceiling light, the thought came unbidden into his head:

Still and all, Peg Leg *was* murdered!

Poor old Peg Leg. What a strange history his had been! He who had so shrunk from any kind of adventure that he had shunned even marriage, the commonest adventure of all, had yet not been able to avoid losing his leg on a three-masted schooner, at Cape Horn, right on the other side of the world.

His longing for peace and quiet had brought him to Jeanneville, from which all human passion seemed excluded, with its houses like dollhouses, and its trees seemingly made of painted wood, like the trees of a toy farm.

And yet, even here, adventure had once more found him out. It had come in sinister guise from a place where he had never so much as set foot, and whose horrors he could barely have imagined. It had come from Place Pigalle, a world apart, a sort of metropolitan jungle, in which the tigers grease their hair and carry Smith & Wessons in their pockets.

One morning, just like any other, with the soft watercolors of sky and landscape all about him, he was gardening, with his straw hat on his head, pricking out his harmless tomato shoots, already seeing them in his mind's eye, perhaps, laden with heavy red fruit, their thin skins splitting in the sunshine, and then, a few minutes later, he was lying dead in his bedroom, which was filled with the wholesome rural smell of polish.

As was her habit, Félicie was eating off the edge of the table, bobbing up every few seconds to take a look at a saucepan simmering on the stove, or to pour boiling water into the coffee percolator. The window was wide open on the deep, velvety blue of a night peppered with stars. Unseen, the crickets chirped to one another, and the frogs croaked in concert. Down in the valley, a train chugged by. In the Anneau d'Or a game of cards was in progress, and good, faithful Lucas was eating cutlets instead of lobster.

"What are you doing?"

"Washing up."

"Not now, child. You're worn out. Do me a favor, will you, and go straight up to bed. . . . Yes! I insist. And don't forget to lock your door."

"I couldn't sleep."

"Is that so? Very well, I'll give you something to help you sleep. . . . Give me a glass of water. . . . I'll just dissolve these two tablets. . . . There . . . Drink up, now. . . . There's nothing to be afraid of. I've no intention of poisoning you."

She drank the draught, to prove to him that she was not

121

afraid. But, irked by Maigret's paternal manner, she felt impelled to reiterate:

"Just the same, I still hate you. One day you'll be sorry for the way you've treated me. . . . Anyway, it doesn't matter, because tomorrow I'm going away."

"Where to?"

"Anywhere . . . I don't ever want to set eyes on you again. I want to get away from this house, and when I've gone, you can do whatever you like."

"As you please. Tomorrow . . ."

"Where are you going?"

"I'm seeing you up to your room. I want to make quite sure you're safely locked in. . . . Oh, good, I see you've closed the shutters. . . . Good night, Félicie."

He returned to the kitchen, to find the carcass of the lobster still lying on a pottery plate. It would remain there, staring at him all through the night.

The hands of the alarm clock on the black mantelpiece stood at half past nine when Maigret took off his shoes and crept silently upstairs, to check that Félicie, under the influence of the Seconol, was sleeping peacefully.

A quarter to ten. Maigret was sitting in Peg Leg's cane armchair. He was smoking his pipe with eyes half shut. The sound of a car coming up the hill. The slam of a door. An oath from Lucas, who had bumped into the bamboo coatrack in the darkness of the hall.

"They've just been on the phone, Chief. . . ."

"Ssh! Keep your voice down. She's asleep."

Lucas looked at the remains of the lobster with the merest hint of resentment.

"The Musician had a girl friend who used the name Adèle. From her file it appears that her real name is Jeanne Grosbois. She was born somewhere near Moulins. . . ."

"Go on."

122

"At the time of the Chamois holdup, she was working in the Tivoli brasserie in Rouen. She left there the day after Pedro was murdered. . . ."

"Presumably she went to join the Musician in Le Havre. What happened next?"

"She spent several months in Toulon, in the Floralies, then she moved to Béziers. . . . She made no secret of the fact that her man was doing time in the Santé."

"Has she been seen in Paris?"

"Yes. Last Sunday . . . One of her old friends spotted her in Place Clichy. She announced that she would soon be leaving for Brazil."

"Is that all?"

"No. The Musician was released last Friday."

All this was just routine, as Maigret called it. At this very moment, police cars were being deployed in the deserted side streets surrounding Place Pigalle. At the Quai, the protesting gentlemen of the fraternity were still being questioned, and were beginning to realize that they had stepped in something very nasty.

"Call and ask them to let us have a photograph of the Musician as soon as possible. There's sure to be one in Records. No, better still, call them and send the taxi to fetch it."

"Anything else, Chief?"

"Yes. When the driver gets back with the photograph, go with it to Poissy, and show it to the man who owns the dance hall near the bridge. It will be closed, of course, so you'll have to wake up the proprietor. . . . He's an ex-con. . . . Show him the photograph and ask him if it's the same man who got into a scuffle with Félicie at his place last Sunday night."

The car drove off. Silence reigned once more. The night was still. Maigret poured brandy into one of the little glasses, warmed it in his hand, and sipped it slowly, glancing up at the ceiling from time to time as he did so.

Every time Félicie turned over in her sleep, the bedspring creaked. Was she dreaming? He wondered whether her dreams were as extravagant as her daytime fantasies.

Eleven o'clock. A clerk in a gray coverall up in the attics of the Palais de Justice extracted two photographs from a file, one taken in profile, the other full face, the features in both pictures being too sharply defined. The clerk handed them to the driver, who had been instructed to take them back to Lucas.

In the neighborhood of Place Pigalle, crowds were pouring out of the Montmartre movie houses and, over their heads, the luminous sails of the Moulin-Rouge rotated. The buses edged their way through the crowds with difficulty. The doormen, in blue, red, and green livery, some dressed as Cossacks, others with black faces, were at their posts outside the various nightclubs, while Superintendent Piaulet, inconspicuous under the trees in the middle of the square, directed operations. All around, unseen by the crowds, his instructions were being carried out.

Janvier was seated at the bar of the Pélican, while the members of the band were taking their instruments out of their cases. In spite of the poor lighting, it did not escape Janvier's notice when a terrified-looking waiter dashed across to the proprietor and dragged him off to the rest room.

Montmartre was full of decent, honest people who had come there for an enjoyable evening out, and were now crowding the café terraces, sipping one last beer before going home to bed. But, on the fringe, the other Montmartre was just beginning to come to life. There, rumors and whispers were rife, and fear was in the air. The proprietor came back from the rest room, smiled at Janvier, went across to a woman sitting alone in a corner, and began talking to her in an undertone.

"I think I'll make an early night of it," she announced. "I'm worn out."

124

She was only one of many who, on hearing that police cars were closing in, preferred not to linger in the danger area. But all the exits were already sealed. On Boulevard Rochechouart, Rue de Douai, Rue Notre-Dame-de-Lorette, dim figures loomed out of the shadows.

"Your papers, please."

What happened next largely depended on the whim of those manning the roadblocks.

"You may go. . . ."

But more often it was:

"Get in. . . ."

Into the dimly lit Black Marias strung out all along the streets.

Had the trap closed yet on the Musician and Adèle, or would they succeed in slipping through the net? Word had certainly reached them. Even if they were cowering in an attic somewhere, some kind soul would have taken the trouble to warn them.

A quarter to twelve. Lucas, who was playing dominoes with the landlord of the Anneau d'Or, to pass the time—only one feeble light had been left on in the deserted bar—heard the taxi draw up outside and got to his feet.

"I shouldn't be gone more than half an hour," he said. "Just time enough to see someone in Poissy, and have a word with the Chief Superintendent afterward."

The dance hall was all in darkness. Lucas's knocks reverberated in the silent night. The first person to appear was a woman in curlers, who poked her head out of a window.

"Fernand . . . it's for you."

Lights, footsteps, grumbling. The door opened a crack.

"Eh? What's that? . . . I thought that little fracas might land me in trouble. . . . I run a respectable business. I've sunk a lot of money in it. The last thing I want is to be mixed up . . ."

125

He shambled over to the bar, his suspenders dangling, his hair uncombed, and studied the two photographs.

"I see. . . . Well, what do you want to know?"

"Is that the man who was put in his place by Félicie?"

"And if it was?"

"Nothing. That's all. Did you know him?"

"Never set eyes on him before or since . . . What's he done?"

Midnight. Lucas got out of the taxi, and Maigret started up out of his armchair like a man roused from sleep. He did not seem greatly interested in what the Sergeant had to tell him.

"I thought as much."

With those jokers, tough nuts though they might be, it was usually plain sailing. One knew the sort of person one was dealing with. One could tell in advance what they would do. Not like that amazing girl Félicie. She was more trouble than the whole lot of them put together.

"What am I to do now, Chief?"

"Go back to Orgeval, and play dominoes while you wait for phone calls."

"Who told you I'd been playing dominoes?"

"You and the proprietor are all alone there, and you don't play cards."

"Are you expecting anything to happen here?"

He shrugged. He didn't know. It didn't matter.

"Good night."

One o'clock in the morning. Félicie was talking in her sleep. Maigret put his ear to her door and tried to hear what she was saying, but was unable to do so. Mechanically he turned the doorknob, and the latch gave.

He smiled. He was touched. She trusted him, after all, it seemed, since she had not troubled to lock her door. He stood for a moment listening to her breathing, and to the words that tumbled out like the babbling of a child. All he could see was the bed, like a milky stain, and her black hair on the pillow. He shut the door softly and returned downstairs on tiptoe.

The shrill blast of a whistle in Place Pigalle. This was the signal. All the exits were sealed. The uniformed police, advancing shoulder to shoulder, scooped up men and women, who were pouring in from all directions in the hope of slipping through the cordon. One policeman was badly bitten on the finger by a fat redhead in evening dress. The Black Marias were filling up.

The proprietor of the Pélican, standing in the doorway of his nightclub, puffing nervously at a cigarette, protested feebly:

"I give you my word, gentlemen, you won't find anything here, other than a few Americans doing the town. . . ."

Young Inspector Dunan, whom Maigret had seen earlier that day in the Hotel Beauséjour, felt someone tugging at his sleeve, and was surprised to recognize the hall porter of the hotel. Come to see the fun, no doubt.

"Hurry! It's her. . . ."

He pointed to the glass door of a café, which was empty except for the proprietor standing behind the bar. At the back of the room a door closed, but not before the Inspector had time to catch a shadowy glimpse of a woman.

"She's the one who came in with a man."

Adèle . . . The Inspector summoned two policemen. They made swiftly for the door at the back, went past the deserted rest rooms and down a narrow staircase, which smelled of damp, stale wine, and urine.

"Open up."

A cellar door. It was locked. One of the men smashed it open with a blow of his shoulder.

"Hands up, whoever is in there."

The beam of a flashlight played over casks, bottles in racks, and crates containing apéritifs. Not a sound was to be heard. Yet as they stood motionless, in response to an order from the Inspector, they sensed, if they did not actually hear, a gasp of indrawn breath and the frantic beating of a heart.

"Get up, Adèle."

She sprang to her feet like a Fury from behind a pile of crates. Knowing that she was trapped, she nevertheless struggled frantically to escape, so that it took all the strength of the three men to fasten handcuffs on her.

"Where's your boyfriend?"

"Don't know."

"What were you doing in this neighborhood?"

"Don't know."

She sniggered.

"It's easier to rough up a defenseless woman than to lay hands on the Musician, isn't it?"

They took her bag from her. In the bar, they opened it, and found nothing but a grubby visiting card, a few small coins, and some letters written in pencil, no doubt those she had received from the Musician during his jail term, since they were addressed to her in Béziers.

The first of the Black Marias, with as many people as it could hold, had driven off toward the Central Police Station. The cells there would soon be overcrowded. Many of the gentlemen were in dinner jackets and the ladies in evening dresses. There were also a number of waiters, and doormen in livery.

"Well, we've got his woman anyway, Superintendent."

Superintendent Piaulet, none too hopeful of getting results, questioned her.

"Sure you won't talk? Where is he?"

"Where you'll never find him."

"Take her away. Not to the cells. Hand her over to Rondonnet."

In the many dubious one-night hotels, police were going

from room to room, asking to see everyone's papers. The men, wearing nothing but their shirts, were highly embarrassed at being found there, especially because they were not alone.

"All I ask is that my wife should not hear of this. . . ."

But, of course, of course!

"Hello! Is that you, Lucas? Would you tell Maigret that we've got Adèle. . . . Yes . . . Needless to say, she won't talk. . . . No, no news of the Musician . . . She's being interrogated, yes. . . . The whole area is still sealed off. . . ."

Now that most of the big fish were in the net, things had quieted down a good deal around Place Pigalle. It was like the flat calm after a storm. The streets were quieter than usual, and late-night revelers coming in from the center of the city were puzzled to find the atmosphere so muted, with even the touts having seemingly lost heart.

Four o'clock. For the third time that night, Lucas went to Cape Horn, to find Maigret divested of his collar and tie.

"You don't happen to have any tobacco on you, do you? I used up the last of mine half an hour ago."

"They've got Adèle. . . ."

"What about him?"

He could still not be absolutely sure that he was right, and yet . . . One fact was incontrovertible: the Musician hadn't a sou to bless himself with. On the night of his release from prison, Adèle had been forced to leave Béziers without the money due her. He had come to Poissy. That was on Sunday. Possibly, he had even come as far as Jeanneville, and followed Félicie to the dance hall. Surely, the easiest way would be to seduce the little, garishly dressed servant girl? He could gain access to the house through her. . . .

But instead, she had slapped his face!

And the following day, Monday, old Lapie was murdered in his bedroom. The Musician had been compelled to flee, empty-handed.

"When did they arrest Adèle?"

"Half an hour ago. They called us immediately."

"You'd better go now, and take the taxi with you."

"Do you think he'll . . . ?"

"Hurry! You must go at once, I tell you."

Maigret shut the door carefully behind him and returned to the kitchen. The red carcass of the lobster was still there on the table. He put out the light and sat down in his chair by the window.

8

A Cup of Coffee for Félicie

She looked about her, wide-eyed. She had no idea what time it was. She had forgotten to set her alarm clock as usual the previous night. It was dark in the bedroom, except for the streaks of silvery daylight showing through the slats of the shutters.

Félicie listened. Her mind was a blank. She still felt dazed and weary, as one does on waking from a very deep sleep. At first, she was unable to distinguish between dream and reality. She had had an argument, a vehement argument, culminating in an actual physical struggle with that detestable, imperturbable man who was bent on destroying her. Oh, how she hated him!

Who had opened her door in the night? Someone had, she was sure. She had lain still, waiting, uneasy. It had been dark. A patch of yellowish light had streamed in from the landing. Then the door had closed. The purring of a car engine . . . All night long, she had heard that sound in her sleep.

She lay very still. She dared not move. She felt that some danger threatened her. There was a weight on her stomach. The lobster. She remembered now. She had eaten too much lobster. She had been drugged. He had forced her to swallow some drug or other.

She listened. What was that? Someone was moving about in the kitchen. She recognized the familiar sound of the coffee grinder. She must be dreaming. Who on earth could possibly be grinding coffee down there?

She gazed down at the floor, all her senses alert. Someone was pouring boiling water. The aroma of freshly made coffee drifted up the staircase right into her room. The clink of china. Another very familiar sound, the sugar canister being opened, and then the slam of a cupboard door.

Someone was coming up the stairs. She suddenly remembered that she had not locked her door last night. Why had she not turned the key? Because her pride would not let her. Yes! She had wanted to show that man that she was not afraid. She had intended to creep out of bed later, after he had gone downstairs, and turn the key without making a sound, but she had fallen asleep as soon as her head had touched the pillow.

Someone was knocking at her door. She raised herself on one elbow. She gazed at the door in anguish, her nerves stretched to breaking point. The knocking was repeated.

"Who's there?"

"Your breakfast."

Frowning, she felt about for her dressing gown, but could not find it, so she quickly slid back into bed and pulled the sheet up to her chin. The door opened, and a tray appeared, with a cloth on it, and a blue-spotted cup.

"Did you sleep well?"

And there was Maigret, looking more imperturbable than ever. He seemed scarcely to be aware that he was in a young girl's bedroom, and that she was still in bed.

"What do you want?"

He put the tray down on the bedside table. He was looking very clean and spruce. Where had he cleaned up? In the kitchen, no doubt, or at the pump. His hair was still damp.

"You do take coffee with milk for breakfast, don't you?

132

Unfortunately, I wasn't able to get to Mélanie Chochoi's for fresh bread. . . . Eat up, child. . . . Here's your dressing gown. I'll turn my back while you put it on."

In spite of herself, she did as she was bidden, and drank a scalding mouthful of coffee. Then, with the cup suspended in midair, she froze.

"Who's that downstairs?"

Someone had moved down there, she was sure of it.

"Who's that downstairs? Tell me!"

"The murderer."

"What did you say?"

She sprang out of bed.

"What's your game this time? You're determined to drive me right around the bend, aren't you? And I'm utterly defenseless. I have no one. . . ."

He sat down on the edge of the bed, watched her helpless flutterings, shook his head and sighed.

"The murderer really is downstairs, you can take my word for it. . . . I was sure he would be back. . . . In his predicament, he had no choice but to take the gamble. . . . Besides which, he thought I was safely out of the way in Paris, directing operations from there. He never dreamed that I was stubbornly determined to keep watch in this house."

"And did he come?"

She stopped short. She was completely at sea. Grasping Maigret by the wrist, she cried:

"But who? Who is he? Surely it isn't possible that . . . ?"

Her eagerness to learn the truth was so great that she dashed out alone to the landing, pale, thin, and shivering, in her vivid-blue dressing gown, intending to go and see for herself. But, suddenly in the grip of fear, she got no farther than the head of the stairs.

"Who is he?"

"Do you still hate me?"

133

"Yes . . . I don't know. . . ."

"Why did you lie to me?"

"Because!"

"Listen to me, Félicie. . . ."

"I'm not going to listen to any more from you. . . . I'm going to open the window and shout for help."

"Why did you never tell me that, when you returned to the house on Monday morning, you saw Jacques Pétillon coming out of the garden? Oh, yes, you did see him. He must just have come through the gate in the hedge. It was on his account that the old man had fetched the bottle of brandy and the two glasses from the sideboard. He thought his nephew had come to make peace, to apologize or something. . . ."

She listened to him in frozen silence, unprotesting.

"And you thought that it was Jacques who had killed his uncle. You found the revolver in the bedroom, and you carried it on your person for three days, before getting rid of it by planting it on a stranger in the Métro. You saw yourself as a heroine of a romance. At all costs, you would save the man you loved—though he, poor fellow, knew nothing about it! And the long and the short of it is that you and your lies very nearly got him arrested for a murder he didn't commit."

"How do you know?"

"Because the real murderer is downstairs."

"Who is he?"

"No one you know."

"You're just trying to trick me again. But I won't say another word, do you hear, not one single word! And now you can take yourself out of here. I want to get dressed. . . . No . . . Stay . . . What could have brought Jacques here, that Monday of all days?"

"He came to oblige the Musician."

"What musician?"

"A buddy of his. You know how it is in Paris. One meets

134

all sorts, some good, some bad. . . . Especially if one happens to play the saxophone in a nightclub . . . If you don't drink your coffee soon, it will be stone cold."

He had opened the shutters earlier. He now went across and looked out the window.

"Hello! There's your friend Léontine on her way to buy her bread. She's looking this way. . . . Little does she know what tales you have to tell her!"

"I won't tell her anything."

"Do you want to bet?"

"I wouldn't dream of such a thing."

"Do you still hate me?"

"Is it true that Jacques is innocent?"

"If I say yes, you won't hate me any longer. If I say no, you'll hate me worse than ever. . . . What a girl! Very well, then. Jacques is guilty of only one thing. One night, a little over a year ago, when he was still living in this house as his uncle's guest, he was guilty, I repeat, of giving shelter for a night, or possibly several nights, to someone whose acquaintance he had made in Montmartre. The man's name was Albert Babeau, alias the Musician, alias Midget. . . ."

"Why Midget?"

"You wouldn't understand. . . . Following a holdup in a nightclub called the Chamois, the Musician, on the run from the police, remembered his friend Pétillon, who had gone to live with an elderly uncle in the country. A splendid hideout for a man on the run . . ."

"I remember now," she exclaimed suddenly.

"What?"

"The only time Jacques . . . the only time he was ever rude to me . . . I had gone into his room without knocking. And I heard a sound, as if something was being hastily pushed out of sight. . . ."

"It wasn't something, it was someone, someone who

135

ought not to have been there. And that someone, before he made his escape from this house, had found an ideal hiding place for his loot, in that same room, under one of the boards on top of the wardrobe. Soon after, he was arrested, and was sentenced to a year in prison. . . . What are you looking at me like that for?"

"It's nothing. . . . Go on."

She was blushing. She looked away, so that the Chief Superintendent would not see the involuntary sparkle of hero worship that had come into her eyes.

"Needless to say, when he was released, penniless, it was imperative for him to lay hands on his loot. His original plan was to gain access to the house by making up to you. . . ."

"Me! Surely you don't imagine that I . . ."

"You slapped his face. . . . His next move was to seek out Pétillon and spin him heaven knows what yarn. Probably that he'd left something he valued behind in the house and needed Pétillon's assistance to get it back. . . . So, while Pétillon was chatting with old Lapie in the garden . . ."

"I see!"

"And about time."

"Thank you very much!"

"It's my pleasure. Peg Leg must have heard something. . . . I daresay he had pretty sharp ears. . . ."

"And how!"

"He went up to his bedroom, and surprised the Musician in the act of climbing on a chair. The man lost his head and shot him at point-blank range. Pétillon, hearing the shot, took to his heels in terror. Meanwhile, the Musician had also fled, but in a different direction. You saw Jacques, your own beloved Jacques, as you would express it, all in capitals, I daresay, but you failed to spot the Musician.

"And that's the whole story. Needless to say, Jacques said

136

not a word. When he realized that he was under suspicion, he lost his head, like the boy that he is. . . ."

"It's not true!"

"Are you suggesting that he's not just a boy? So be it. Then he's an idiot. Instead of coming to me with the whole story, he got it into his head that he must seek out the Musician and demand an explanation. He went looking for him in every sleazy dive he could think of. At last, in despair, he even went as far as Rouen, in the hope of getting some information out of the man's mistress. . . ."

"How did he come to know a woman like that?" interrupted Félicie, stung by jealousy.

"That I can't tell you, my dear. In Paris, you know . . . Anyway, he had worked himself up into a fearful state. He was at the end of his rope. . . . That night, he had reached the point where he had to tell someone or burst, but before he could do so, the Musician, who had friends to keep him informed, shot him, to teach him to keep his mouth shut."

"Don't talk like that."

"That same night, the Musician came back here, hoping that this time he would find what he was looking for. You can't imagine the predicament of a man on the run without money. He searched the cavity on top of the wardrobe, but found nothing. . . . You, on the other hand, were left with a tangible memento of his visit. . . . He reasoned that, if the money was not here, then Pétillon must have found it, which explains why he sent Adèle to search his room on Rue Lepic.

"But nothing was found there either. . . . That same night, Montmartre was completely sealed off by a police cordon. The man was trapped like a hunted animal. Adèle was caught.

"God alone knows how he did it, but the Musician managed to slip through the police cordon. By now, he was more desperate than ever, and there is no one more desperate

137

than a hardened criminal on the run. He took a taxi to Poissy. He was so broke that, by way of payment, he coshed the taxi driver on the back of the head."

Félicie shivered. She was gazing at Maigret as if watching the breath-taking denouement of a suspense movie.

"Did he come here?"

"He did. . . . Very cautiously, without making a sound. He didn't so much as tread on a twig as he crossed the garden and crept past the open kitchen window, and . . ."

To her, Maigret had already become a hero of romance. She marveled at him.

"Did he attack you?"

"No. When he was least expecting it, he suddenly felt the cold steel of a revolver barrel against his temple."

"What did he do?"

"Nothing. He just said:

" 'Hell! I've copped out!' "

She felt let down. But no, it couldn't possibly have been as easy as all that. Her old mistrust flooded back; her features sharpened.

"Are you sure you're not hurt?"

"I've just told you. . . ."

He was only saying that to reassure her! Of course there had been a struggle. He was a hero, and . . .

Suddenly she caught sight of the tray on the bedside table.

"And after all that, you quietly set about grinding the coffee. . . . You had the . . . the presence of mind to prepare my breakfast coffee, remembering that I took it with milk, and bring it up to me. . . ."

She was on the verge of crying. . . . Then she wept tears of gratitude and hero worship.

"You did all that, you! But why? Tell me why?"

"Why indeed? Because I hate you. I hate you so much that, as soon as Lucas gets here with the taxi, I will be off, taking my sausage with me. . . . Oh! I forgot to tell you that the Musician is tied up like a sausage. I had to borrow poor Lapie's gardening twine for the purpose."

"And what of me?"

It was all he could do to repress a smile at this cry, which, whether she knew it or not, came from the bottom of her heart.

It meant: What of me? Am I to be left all alone? Am I never again to know what it is to be taken seriously? Will there no longer be anyone to harass me with questions, and tease me and . . . ?

And what of me?

"You'll have to make do with Jacques. . . . That shop in the Faubourg-Saint-Honoré where you can buy grapes and oranges and champagne will still be there. . . . I can't remember now what the visiting hours are at the hospital, but you can easily find out. . . ."

The taxi, such a familiar sight in Paris but looking somewhat out of place on the winding roads of these parts, with fields on either side, came into view.

"You'd better hurry up and get dressed."

He went out to the landing, without so much as a backward glance, and as he began going downstairs, he heard her murmur:

"How can you be so horrid to me?"

A few seconds later, he was skirting old Lapie's armchair, in which the Musician was securely tied up. Overhead, footsteps came and went, water splashed, coat hangers rattled in a wardrobe, a shoe was dropped and picked up, and a voice could be heard muttering feverishly.

Félicie was there, all right!

L'Aiguillon-sur-Mer, 1942

139